DEPARTURES
SCOTT COLE

BLACKTSHIRT

BOOKS

"Greetings from Trammel Beach" originally appeared in
Beach Bodies: A Beach Vacation Horror Anthology, 2022.

"The Trunk" originally appeared in
Blackberry Blood: A Dark Selection of Poetry and Fiction, 2021.

"The Penanggalan" originally appeared in
Worst Laid Plans: An Anthology of Vacation Horror, 2020.

ALSO BY SCOTT COLE

Crazytimes

Triple Axe

Slices: Tales of Bizarro and Absurdist Horror

SuperGhost

EGG HOUSE

The egg was a surprise, to say the very least.

I hadn't noticed it during the open house, nor the inspection, nor the final walkthrough on the morning of closing. I never even spotted it during my first few weeks living in the house.

When Spring arrived suddenly, ushering the cold air out of town overnight, I decided to follow in my mother's admittedly traditional footsteps and give my new home a proper cleaning, floor to ceiling.

Truthfully, I should have done this between signing the papers and moving in, but a disagreement with my former landlord meant an abrupt exit from my previous rental while I was at the tail end of the homebuying process, and instead of having a month overlap between homes, I had to move into the house immediately.

I suppose I did have time to clean upon my arrival. But I chose not to, having fallen into a sort of depression in the wake of my swift eviction from the apartment, the emotional whirlwind of purchasing a house for the first time in my life, and the shock of losing my job the day of my closing—something I was informed of over the phone when I called in to let my supervisor (whom, at the time, I also considered a friend) know the process had gone smoothly.

So, for several weeks, my routine was simply: wake up, eat, laze about, avoid human interaction, nap, listen intently to music with eyes closed, eat again (sometimes), fret, go back to sleep.

Sometimes I would stand and stare out the window, usually at my backyard, which was simultaneously overgrown and pathetically malnourished, with slumping heaps of tall, dead grass.

Eventually, though, my funk began to dissipate, and I began to feel somewhat more like myself. I decided to wake up at the same time each morning, prepare three well-balanced meals per day, start an exercise routine, and put some effort into searching for a new job. Perhaps I would take a class, I thought, given the surplus of spare hours I had.

And I decided it was time I get my house in order.

I began in the kitchen, which seemed to be the filthiest room in the house, certain corners crusted over with the remnants of meals from who knows how many years prior. There were numerous patches of dried residue on the counters, and crumbs inside the cabinets. In one corner of the stovetop I even found a small pile of yellow crumbles—a material somehow both chalky and gelatinous, which had a vague resemblance to the yolk of a hard-boiled egg. All along the baseboards I found dustings of old meals, and small mounds of black, gray, and white specks, which looked almost, but not quite, like hills of salt and pepper. There were spatters on the backsplash and smears on the walls far too high for any food to rightfully be.

It was almost uncanny; I simply hadn't noticed the amount of grime present on any of my first several visits to the place. In fact, it had seemed spotless during the open house. And the home inspector I contracted after my offer had been accepted even remarked at how easy the owners had made his job, keeping everything in such fantastic shape. I now wonder if the previous owners paid him off to say nice things and sign paperwork that would have otherwise been torn up.

The floors of most of the rooms in the house were dirty as well. As I began to sweep, vacuum, and mop, I came to realize that the floors were actually completely different colors than I had initially thought. There were loose splinters of wood and bits of what appeared to be straw, or perhaps rope fibers, collected beneath the radiators. Embedded in the plush carpeting of one room, I found several bits of dried leaves, no doubt having fallen from the treads of filthy shoes.

The bathrooms were a mess too. Foul-colored smears adorned the tiles, white and yellow spatters covered the mirrors, and the tub in the main bathroom was soiled with brown and orange stains I chose not to think too deeply about.

It was only after giving the bathroom a full cleaning that I discovered the egg. It was hidden behind the door that separated the facilities from the main bedroom—a door that had remained open against the bedroom wall since I moved in.

Upon finishing in the bathroom, I had decided to start wiping down the bedroom baseboards, which led me to close the door in question. When I did, I was astonished by what I found.

The egg was quite large—I couldn't imagine what had birthed it—not to mention the fact that it seemed too big to fit behind the door. It had easily as much volume as the nightstand beside the bed—and yet, somehow, the egg was able to tuck into the space behind the door with plenty of room. Examining the area there led to the discovery that despite looking flat, the wall actually curved in a concave fashion, allowing more space behind the door than one might expect or even observe from a distance. Some of these old houses, in my experience, seemed averse to right angles and flat surfaces.

The egg itself had a relatively smooth texture, though it felt more leathery than shell-like. There were inconsistent ripples which I would not have expected to see—although, to be honest, I had never spent much time examining eggs very closely. Its color was a gray-brown and mottled with both darker and lighter flecks and splotches, and its shape was slightly tapered near the top, as most eggs are.

To say I was unnerved by the notion that this egg had apparently been in my bedroom the entire time would be an understatement. I wondered how I could have missed such a thing for as long as I had.

Granted, I hadn't slept in my bed every night. I had often fallen asleep on the couch downstairs. And I hadn't bothered to shower every day, which limited the number of times I passed through the doorway in question.

But beyond that, what sort of monstrous bird could have laid an egg so large? Surely something that big could not hide in plain sight. And how could it have infiltrated the house? A bird the size I was envisioning would not have been able to fit through an open window, and probably would have had trouble squeezing through a door—unless the bird had been the previous owners' pet, and one which stayed inside all the time. But if that had been the case, wouldn't there have been some evidence of its existence during that initial tour, or the inspection process? It was quite the mystery.

Eventually I resigned myself to the fact that I had been deeply depressed for weeks, and obviously hadn't been thinking clearly about anything. Missing things right in front of my nose was not terribly surprising when I stopped to think about it.

The question became what to do about it now.

I didn't know much about birds, or how moving the egg could affect what was inside it—not to mention what it might mean to the mother. Had I already gone too far by touching the leathery outside? Would the egg now be abandoned? Would the baby bird inside be shunned? I had to give some thought to what was next.

I supposed the egg wasn't harming anything by staying where it was. With the door opened against the wall, the thing was hidden. I didn't even notice it. Until I had a solution that made sense, I decided to leave it be.

That night, I did sleep in my bed. I did not recall any dreams, but it was the first night in a while I slept straight through without interruption.

Upon waking the next morning, I noticed a sour

scent in the air. I had somehow, temporarily forgotten about the egg, and wondered if the odor was related to the fact that I had not yet done a load of laundry since moving in. I gathered my clothes in a basket and carried them to the basement.

The light down there flickered, reminding me I needed to replace it. I wasn't sure I had any spare bulbs, though. I realized I might have to venture out, but thankfully there was a shop just down the street that might have what I needed. I was running low on cleaning supplies anyway.

As the wash got underway, I retreated back upstairs and set my mind toward breakfast. I absentmindedly brewed coffee and, completely missing the irony, prepared an omelet. By the time my breakfast had been made and eaten, it was time to go back to the basement and switch the laundry over. The dryer door creaked like a squawking, angry bird, reminding me of the conundrum in my bedroom.

I spent some time trying to come up with a solution. I considered moving the egg as delicately as possible to the backyard. There were trees there, and tall, albeit dead, grasses. And the area, while not large, was fenced in, offering some level of protection. While the egg would no longer be inside the house, it would be close, and I could keep an eye on it while the mother bird was away.

I tried to think about the best way to transport the egg. Since the surface felt unlike a typical eggshell, it was tough for me to determine how prone to damage it might be in the process. There was a hand truck in the basement— something the previous owners had left behind. I considered padding it with a few blankets to form a sort of nest and using that to move the egg. I wondered if it would be soft enough to cushion the egg from breaking as I rolled the hand truck down the stairs one by one, or if this was all simply a recipe for disaster.

I went back upstairs. The room still reeked, and it finally dawned on me that the smell was not from my unwashed clothes, but from the thing behind the door. As I approached the egg, the odor intensified, and as I pulled the door away from the wall, I could see that it now sat in a small puddle of greenish-yellow slime. Perhaps it had been there before, but I surely hadn't noticed. And the egg itself now seemed to be sweating, its shell covered in a thin sheen of the same substance.

I sat down on the floor beside it, careful not to touch the slime. At the time it didn't even occur to me how the gooey substance might affect the finish of the floorboards.

I heard a low rumble, which immediately evoked memories of distant thunder, but I quickly realized the sound wasn't coming from outside, but instead from within the egg. It didn't seem to be moving, though—a small thing for which I was thankful.

I felt the time had come to move the egg. I no longer wanted it inside my house. I wondered if it was suddenly showing signs of disease and feared what might happen next. Perhaps the mother bird had recognized this early on and abandoned the egg here to wither away out of sight. But if that was the case, I wondered why the interior of my home was the chosen place.

I was afraid to touch it now. I tried to remember if I had a pair of work gloves—and if not, where my winter gloves were stored. I still had plenty of items in boxes from my move several weeks prior—boxes I had let sit untouched during my depressive stretch.

It was in that moment that the egg groaned again, and this time did move. The shell suddenly expanded outward in my direction, swelling like a balloon and creaking like a pair of new boots, but it could only grow so much before reaching its breaking point—which is exactly what happened next.

I stood up and moved back a step or two as the wall of the egg split open softly. A few spatters of slime hit the wall, but the movement was more like a pair of lips parting than any sort of explosion. A jagged vertical line formed midway down the side before spreading to the tapered top and rounder bottom. I heard another low rumble next, but then, silence. Just as suddenly as the egg had split, everything went still.

After a momentary pause, I decided to move closer again, and dropped to one knee directly in front of the crack in the egg. Through the new seam, I tried to look deeper in. Was the baby bird inside okay? Or would I immediately be taking the egg and its contents out to the trash? The stench was still quite vile.

I angled myself so as not to block the light, but still had trouble seeing inside. I spotted the glint of what I assumed was an eye, but little else. I slid closer, finding myself overwhelmed with curiosity.

I cleared my throat in an effort to arouse some movement from within, but when there still was none, I decided I would make contact with the egg once again after all.

Foregoing my gloves, I reached toward the egg, several inches to the side of the new opening, and touched it lightly with the tip of one finger. When there was no movement or sound, I touched it again with two, somewhat more forcefully. Again, there was nothing.

After some hesitation, the urge to see what was inside took over completely, and I knew what I must do. I snuck my fingers into either side of the opening and pulled the edges apart.

I was not prepared for what I would find.

The egg offered some resistance, but I was able to spread the opening wider without too much effort. Just inside the shell was a layer, several inches thick, of some sort of insulation. It seemed to be made of something like cotton, but stickier, almost like hundreds of spider webs all stratified together to form a dense mass of cushioning. But beyond this material was the strangest part of all.

As the insulation spread and split apart, I was able to see into the center of the egg. To say I was surprised would understate the uncanniness of what I found, and my ability to comprehend it. But I stared for several moments and ultimately realized that yes, there was indeed a miniature house inside the egg.

I was struck with memories from my childhood, of my mother toying with her own childhood dollhouse in the attic. She had held onto it in the hopes of passing it on to her own offspring one day. But once I was of an appropriate age, I had no interest in such things. She had kept it in the attic anyway, hoping I might someday change my mind, or that perhaps she might eventually have another child who would want it.

This house inside the egg reminded me of that one somewhat, although they were not too similar.

This house seemed to be made with more natural

materials, instead of compressed wood and plastics. The walls of this house appeared to be made of tree bark and feathers. The floors and ceilings were thatched, using twigs and straw. There were tiny pieces of furniture constructed of bone and sticks, accoutrements of shell and beak, edges wrapped in leaves and bits of twine, and a roof ensconced in moss.

There were seven rooms in total, including the half-height attic space near the tapered top of the egg.

Another rumbling sound erupted nearby, but it wasn't from the egg this time. It seemed to come from somewhere else inside my house; I could feel vibrations through the floorboards. But I was so taken with the smaller house inside the egg, the sound didn't register at first.

I stared inside, taking in all the miniature details of each room. There was a chair made from what appeared to be a tiny rib cage, a countertop of small stones, a bench of twisted twigs—even portraits hanging on the walls, though I wasn't able to discern who was depicted, or if they were human, avian, or something else.

My house shook again as another deep roar emanated through it. This time the noise and vibration captured my attention. It was like an earthquake. But just before taking my eyes off the tiny house, I spotted something especially odd within. In one of the rooms, just behind a door, sat an unusual-looking egg. Just like the one in my bedroom, this egg's scale seemed too large for the space it occupied, rising about half the height of the door behind which it was partially hidden.

And for a second I thought I saw it move.

I stood to my feet as the house continued to shake.

Dust trickled down from the walls and ceiling. Broken bits of plaster skittered inside the walls. Wooden joints groaned.

And just then, an excruciatingly loud squawk rattled my eardrums. Instantly I knew it was the mother bird, screeching from above. Where was she, I wondered—in the attic?

As I backed away from the egg and the little house inside it, I saw the smaller egg behind the tiny door expand and ooze. As another shriek from the mother bird sounded, I saw a vertical seam form down the side of the little egg as it began to split open.

At that point, I ran. I didn't think about it; my legs simply carried me away. I took nothing with me but what I was wearing, and I dashed down the steps, two or three at a time, and out the front door.

When I reached the street and turned the corner, at the edge of my vision, I could have sworn I saw the two slopes of the house's roof flap like a pair of wings. I may have screamed. I certainly didn't stare or linger. I turned my head completely away from the house and continued running, never looking back. I ran until I could no longer hear the squawking of the mother bird or feel the vibrations from its violent calls.

I was in the next town before I stopped, slicked with sweat, exhausted and bewildered.

Somehow, before I collapsed, I located a small, run-down hotel and, with minimal words, I managed to rent a room. Once inside, I threw the locks and immediately checked behind every door. The accommodations were sparse and rather dingy, but I didn't care. Once I was convinced of my safety, I crawled into the bed and cocooned myself in the covers, hoping the mattress was not infested with anything.

I remain here to this day, my savings dwindling. I don't go out much. I don't speak to anyone. I am still fearful. But I believe I am relatively safe.

I try not to think of my old house too often, but it's difficult to keep it entirely out of my mind. The image of that tiny egg in the house in the egg in the house, and what miniature horror might have been inside it, haunts me still.

GREETINGS FROM
TRAMMEL BEACH

"Sunblock...sunblock..."

Andrew digs through a bag, shifting and sliding its contents around without actually removing anything, and eventually finds what he's after. He pulls the plastic tube out and drops it into a smaller bag—the one they'll be taking to the beach.

"Okay, are you all ready?"

Kayleigh and Conor both look up from their phones, WTF expressions on their faces—the kind their father is used to seeing. Kayleigh is on the chair by the desk, a small shoulder bag at her feet and a long t-shirt over her swimsuit, while Conor sits on the edge of the mattress, bouncing a knee, rustling his own swimsuit, making the entire bed shake.

"We've *been* ready," Kayleigh responds, speaking for herself and her brother.

"Shan, how about you? Almost ready to go?"

Shannon angles her head out from the bathroom and extends a fist with her thumb pointed upward. Her other hand is working a toothbrush, and her lips are ringed with white foam.

Ten minutes later, they step onto the sand under a wooden arch with the words "Trammel Beach" carved into it. It's only a short walk from their rooms, and the view is stunning.

That must be why the island is named Bellavista, Andrew supposes, although he swears he could've come up with a dozen better names for it, back when he worked in marketing. He had to leave that job years ago, though, while he still had some semblance of a soul remaining. It was killing him.

Still, Andrew thinks, the generic name for this place doesn't take anything away from the beauty of their surroundings.

The sand is nearly pure white, the water a gorgeous, almost unnatural turquoise with jagged white edges as soft waves roll in. There are black rocks in the distance to the right, where the beach curves against the water's edge. To the left, palm trees bend toward the water between thatched-roof cabanas.

Everywhere Andrew looks, people are sunbathing or playing. Squealing children are splashing in the water. A group of twenty-somethings are playing volleyball. A woman is tossing a red frisbee for her dog to fetch.

"Wow," Shannon says, lifting up the brim of her big, floppy, straw-colored hat and feeling the warmth of the sun on her cheeks. "What a view! And could it be a more perfect day?"

It's already crowded, but there are still a few good spots available by the looks of things.

"God, I can't believe how we lucked out," Shannon continues. "This place is gorgeous. Looks like a postcard!"

That was, in fact, how they discovered Bellavista. A postcard had landed in their mailbox, due to the sender mistakenly writing the wrong address on it. The picture side of the card displayed a stunning photo of these same white sands and brilliant waters, with the words "Greetings from Trammel Beach" emblazoned across it. Shannon had been so taken by the beauty of the image that she had decided to look the place up online while planning the family's next vacation. In doing so she had stumbled upon a deal they couldn't possibly pass up.

"Oh, that reminds me," Kayleigh interjects. "Is there a gift shop here or something? I need to send Amanda a postcard."

"How Old World of you," Shannon teases. "Why not just text her a picture?"

"I just tried, but it won't go through. Maybe I can send it when we go back to the room. But anyway, there's something kind of romantic about getting a postcard in the mail, don't you think?"

"I do, actually. That's sweet. We can ask the concierge when we head back later."

"Cool."

They find a spot, lay out some towels, and set up a couple chairs.

"Let's go in," Conor says impatiently to his sister, and

they run for the water. Shannon and Andrew stay back to settle into their portable chairs and soak up some sun.

Shannon grabs the tube of sunblock and squirts some onto her arms and legs before spreading it around. She wears a dark blue one-piece swimsuit, the kind that's meant more for fashion than getting wet. She has no plans to enter the water, at least not beyond her ankles.

"I would've rubbed that in for you, you know," Andrew says with a smirk. "All you had to do was ask."

"Oh, I didn't want to ask. I like a man who takes control," she responds, flirting. "Too bad you missed your shot, but...who knows, maybe there will be other opportunities... later tonight."

Andrew smiles. He can't see his wife's eyes behind her dark sunglasses, but he knows the look she's flashing, and it's a deviously sexy one. As much as he loves the beach, he's already looking forward to the sun going down.

"You want some?" she asks. Andrew keeps his smile going and adds a crooked eyebrow to the look. "The sunblock, you beast!" she clarifies, and they both laugh.

"I'm good, thanks. Need to work on my tan a bit."

"Ha! Your tan looks perfect!"

"I dunno, I think it could be a little *more* perfect."

"Show-off," Shannon says. "I wish I had those auto-tan genes. But no, my parents both had to be the fairest of the fair-skinned, didn't they?"

Andrew just chuckles.

"Kayleigh and Conor are lucky they inherited that quality from you, instead of my hideous glow-in-the-dark paleness. I mean, have you ever gotten a single sunburn in your entire life?"

Andrew doesn't answer with words. He just shakes his head no, then tucks his hands behind his head and leans back.

Shannon leans back too, inhaling the sea air and exhaling deeply with a moan of contentment. Seagulls fly overhead, squawking as they search for a late morning meal.

"So, Kayleigh and Amanda seem to be getting very close," Andrew says.

"Seems that way. They've been spending a lot of time together. Mostly at Amanda's house, from what Kayleigh tells me. She also tells me Amanda's mom is there all the time, but I seriously doubt that."

Andrew scoffs and sighs. *Ah, young love,* he thinks to himself. He settles even deeper into his seat and smiles at the sun above.

A few minutes later, Shannon pulls a well-worn, dog-eared paperback from the bag.

Andrew hears her rifling among the sounds of the waves, the birds, and the other beachgoers. He cracks one eye open and peeks but can't tell what she's got.

"Something trashy, I assume?"

"You know me too well."

•••••••••••••

"Bwahahahaha!" Conor screams as his head pops above the surface with a splash. He raises his arms out of the water and Kayleigh squeaks at the sight. They're covered in dark green seaweed, which he has wrapped around his hands, wrists, and forearms. Loose ends dangle off him like the tattered linen wraps of an ancient horror movie mummy.

"Raaahhhhhhhr," he growls and feints toward her, the water restricting his movement somewhat.

Kayleigh makes a disgusted sound. "So gross."

Conor is only two years younger than his sister, but their maturity levels feel three or four times that to her. She's grown a lot in the past year or two, emotionally and physically. She's graduated from childhood to young womanhood. She's even begun falling in love.

Soon, she'll have to start thinking about, and looking at, colleges. For now, though, she's happy to enjoy this family vacation, even if her brother is a bit of a goofball. She'll be happy to get home to see Amanda too. She wonders if the postcard she plans to send later will arrive before or after she returns home.

"I'm getting out for a minute," she says. "You coming or staying here?"

"I'll stay."

"Okay. I need to go ask Mom something. Be careful with the undertow."

Conor brings a seaweed-wrapped hand to his forehead and offers his sister a formal salute.

"Eww."

Kayleigh makes her way to the edge of the water and crawls out, raising both hands up to squeeze the water from her long dark hair. As she does this, moving from water to wet sand to dry, she feels the stares of the boys and men around her, gazing at her bikini-clad body, which has only recently filled out to a form that displays a handful of years beyond her true age. She's unsure how she feels about this newfound attention, but she has an urge to get back to her parents' basecamp before anyone approaches her.

•••••••••••

"I told you that bikini was going to get her some looks."

"Relax, Andrew, she's sixteen."

"I know, but she looks twenty-one. And all the people staring...I don't like it."

"If she feels comfortable, let her wear what she wants. Besides, no man is getting anywhere near her, trust me."

Just as Shannon says the words, a teenage boy approaches Kayleigh. She ignores him, expertly turning her head one way while shifting her path to the opposite direction. The kid, already stumbling over his words, trips over his own feet too and nearly falls over. Embarrassed, he rights himself and walks back to his friends, who are flopping on the sand with laughter. Their parents look around, trying to figure out the cause of the commotion.

"Hey," Kayleigh says as she makes it back to where her parents are stationed. She quickly grabs a towel to wrap around herself. "I had trouble finding you. The undertow pulled us farther than I thought."

"What are you thinking about lunch?" Andrew asks.

"I was just coming to ask you," says Kayleigh. "Conor's playing with seaweed and it's totally disgusting, but it also kind of made me want sushi."

"That's two votes for sushi," Shannon says, turning to Andrew with a wide smile. "I bet my darling son will give us the majority."

•••••••••••

Conor dives underwater to gather more seaweed. He wraps it around his arms while still beneath the surface, then grabs a handful of wet sand from the ocean floor and floats back up. Above water, he rubs the sand into the vegetation he's collected, applying it like a visual effects artist to both arms. The monster flesh he's created would look great on camera, he thinks.

About a half hour has passed from the time Kayleigh left him, but it feels like only moments to Conor, as he dreams of someday working in the movies. He wonders if he'll be able to recreate this look at home. Maybe he can convince his mom to pick up some seaweed at the Asian supermarket downtown.

Eventually, Kayleigh returns to retrieve her brother. She's put her long t-shirt back over her swimsuit now, but still feels plenty of staring eyes. Conor notices that her hair is mostly dry as she beckons him out of the water. Somehow she convinces him to unfurl his stinky, slimy ocean floor adornments before they return to where their parents are stationed.

They help their parents pack up the chairs and shake sand from the towels, placing most of their things in the bags they brought with them. As they do so, two seagulls land nearby and putter about the sand. One of them has something hanging out of its beak. Something wet and slimy, and pink.

"Aww, yuck," Conor says with a smile. "I wonder what kind of fish that was."

Andrew attempts to shoo the seagulls away, but they don't scare off easily. Clearly they feel some sense of ownership over this beach, Andrew thinks. He doesn't blame them. He and his family are just tourists, but this is home for the birds.

"Okay, gang, let's drop this stuff at the room and then we'll go find food," he says as they start back.

"Sushi," Shannon says.

The sand is hot. Their feet sink and shift with each step, and Conor complains that his toes are getting burned, but Shannon tells him he's going to be fine. She steps on the edge of a broken shell as she says this, but stifles any reaction.

"I'm dying for a dragon roll," Kayleigh says. "We haven't gotten sushi in forever."

"*Staaaaaaaay.*"

"Huh?" says Kayleigh, looking at her dad.

He looks back at her, confused. "I didn't say anything."

Kayleigh's eyes shift to her brother, but he looks just as confused. A screeching seagull passes right over their heads at just that moment, and Kayleigh jumps, startled. Conor laughs.

It feels like it takes forever to get off the beach.

"I didn't realize we walked this far in," Shannon says.

Andrew agrees. "Maybe there's an undertow out here too."

Finally, after what feels like fifteen minutes, they reach the edge of the sand, and pass under the Trammel Beach arch again, where they find the path that takes them almost directly to the doors to their adjoined rooms.

"Well, I'm definitely hungry now," says Conor, out of breath. "What a workout."

•••••••••••••

"Can I take a quick shower before we go to lunch?" Kayleigh asks. Shannon and Andrew look across the room at each other like they're waiting for the other one to respond. Conor flops himself down on the cushy chair in the corner of the room, annoyed about any further delay.

"Uhh, sure, honey. Everything okay?" Shannon finally offers after a pause.

"Yeah, I'm just covered in this saltwater, I guess. I feel gross. Probably should've hit the shower at the beach, but I wasn't thinking."

"We can wait a few minutes," Andrew says. "No problem."

"Thanks. I'll be quick." Kayleigh disappears through the side doorway and heads into the bathroom in the adjoining room she's sharing with Conor. The bathroom door clicks shut and the water starts, muffled behind the barriers of the bathroom and shower doors.

"Have you seen a gift shop or anything around here?" Shannon asks Andrew. She feels an itch on her leg and looks down to swat whatever is crawling on her, but instead finds a patch of sand stuck to her calf. She swipes twice to brush it off. "Kayleigh wanted to pick up a postcard to send to Amanda."

"Oww! *Dammit!*" Andrew exclaims, though not in response to anything his wife has said. Conor perks up, startled, while Shannon steps toward her husband.

"What is it?"

"I don't know. Just felt a twinge or something on the back of my neck. *Owwww!*"

"Here, let me take a look," Shannon says. Andrew sits on the edge of the bed, one hand on his neck, as Shannon positions herself over him.

"I'll be back in a minute," Conor says, excusing himself to use his parents' bathroom, not that they notice. He tugs at his swimsuit in mid-stride in an attempt to undo the twist that formed upon sitting in the oversized chair.

"Oh, honey," Shannon says, pulling back Andrew's collar to examine his neck. "You're not going to believe this."

"What, did I get bit or something? Cut?"

"Nope. But I've got some news about your perfect complexion, buddy. You may have finally outgrown it." She smiles slightly, even though she knows it's wrong to take any delight in this discovery.

"Huh? What are you talking about?" Andrew stands up and moves to the mirror over the desk, across the room from the bed. He pulls his collar away from his neck, just as Shannon had, and tries to bend in such a way that he's able to see whatever she saw. It's a struggle, but he recognizes the problem right away.

Sunburn. He's actually sunburned. For the first time.

"Guess you should've taken me up on that sunblock after all, huh?" Shannon says. She tries to flatten her smile, but she's unsuccessful.

"Oh, what are you laughing at? I can't believe this. I've never gotten a sunburn in my life! My mom used to say I was even tan as a baby!"

"I'm sorry, honey. Hey, before we get lunch, let's look for that gift shop. We can get Kayleigh's postcard, and maybe they can tell us where we to find some aloe gel or something."

"Fine. *Ahh!*"

"Well, don't *touch* it. Oh, actually, we should just ask the concierge where we can pick this stuff up, so we don't waste time roaming around. I'm starving. Bet you are too."

In the other room, the hiss of Kayleigh's shower comes to a stop.

Shannon feels another itch, this time on her other leg, and looks down to find more sand stuck to her.

"Shit, maybe I should've gotten a quick shower too." She rubs at the sand, but it doesn't move. "What the—?"

"Are you about finished in there, Conor?" Andrew says. But Conor doesn't answer, at least not at first. "Conor? You alright, buddy?"

There's a pause. And then, finally, a quiet voice from the other side of the door. "Something's wrong."

Again Andrew and Shannon flash looks at each other. What could this be about, they both wonder. Shannon goes to just outside the door.

"I'm right here, honey. What's up?" As she says this, she finds still more sand stuck to the inside of her left forearm. And again it won't budge. She brushes at it with her fingers, then the heel of her opposite hand, but it's as if she smeared a glue stick on herself before going to the beach.

Without another word, the bathroom door cracks open and Shannon slips in before closing it again.

Kayleigh returns to the room, flustered. She's dressed, but wipes her arms intently with a towel. "Is this place, like, what they mean by 'hard water'? Amanda said they had that where they used to live. I feel all slimy. Like I can't get clean."

"Hey, give us a second, okay?" Andrew says, meeting her at the adjoining doorway. "Something's up with your brother."

"What, does this place have those little fish that swim up your urethra too? He deserves it. You should've seen what he was doing in the water earlier. So gross." Kayleigh can tell her father thinks she's funny but can't laugh because sometimes that's the way parents have to be. "Wait, are you sunburned, Dad?"

"Andrew? Can you come here?" Shannon sounds concerned, but she's clearly holding back, probably so she doesn't make Conor any more nervous than he already is. Kayleigh can hear his whining through the bathroom door, like he's having a panic attack or something. Like he's on the verge of tears.

"Oh my god, Dad, you're bright red! Is that a *blister* on your neck?"

Andrew's attention has already shifted back to his wife and son. He strides toward the bathroom, while Kayleigh stays where she is. She continues using the towel, now on her legs, wiping up and down, somewhat vigorously, trying to feel cleaner, but it's no use.

She sees something when her father opens the door to where her mother and brother are. Conor's standing there, leaning back against the sink, with the bottom edge of his trunks pulled all the way up to his hip on one side. There's something on his leg. Something dark green, almost black, and kind of slimy looking. Just like the seaweed he was messing with out in the water.

Andrew closes the door halfway and Kayleigh hears her mother say something like *"It won't come off!"* and suddenly things seem much more serious.

"Is everything okay?" Kayleigh calls across the room.

"It's fine," Shannon responds. "We'll be out in a minute. Get your shoes on."

Without a word, Kayleigh grabs a pair of flats from

her and Conor's room, and returns to their parents' room, where she sits on the swivel chair by the desk and slides them on. She sits and waits, nervous about whatever's going on in the bathroom.

What could it be? Conor was playing in the seaweed, but really, *what could have happened out there?* Maybe some weird little fish really did swim up his shorts and got stuck up there. Maybe it got snagged on some seaweed and everything got all tangled up? *Boys are such a mess*, she thinks. She wonders if everything truly is going to be okay.

Just then, she hears movement. The bathroom door opens and something bangs against the inside of it. She hears her mom gasp. She hears Conor whimper. And she hears something not unlike the scratching of sandpaper.

The door opens further, and her dad slumps out, like he's sitting on the floor and suddenly decided to lay down for nap. His head hits the doorframe on the way through, then falls all the way to the carpet just outside the door, by the closet.

Kayleigh gasps and stands up, though she's unsure what to do.

"*Kayleigh? Kay?*" It's her mother calling out. "I need some help here, honey." Shannon steps out from the bathroom, looking haggard, like she's aged twenty years since Kayleigh left to take a shower.

Her mom stands there, rubbing her arms against each other like she's got a rash. Only it's nothing like that. Her arms look like they're covered in sand. She scratches at her legs too, clawing at them like an animal. Kayleigh sees how they look the same as her arms.

"Mom? What's going on? Are you okay? What's

wrong with Dad?"

"Daddy's gonna be okay, honey. He just got a little sunburn and needs to rest for a few minutes."

"Oh my god! Conor? Are you okay?"

"He's going to be fine too, Kayleigh. Listen, I need you to call someone, okay?"

Kayleigh acts immediately, and moves toward the phone on the end table, but her legs seem to simultaneously stick to each other and also slip apart. She loses her balance and falls to her knees. She reaches out with both arms to break her fall, but her palms just slide across the carpet like it's made of ice, and she lands on her chin.

There's a wet, sloppy sound in the bathroom. The noise startles Shannon, and she leaps away from the doorway when she sees what it is.

From where Kayleigh is on the floor, struggling to get back up, she sees something dark green reach out from the bathroom. Several somethings, actually. A series of wet, ragged arms curl themselves around the doorframe like the arms of an octopus. They grasp the edges and pull. The vegetation quickly reaches out even further, to the corner on the opposite end of the closet where it turns toward the main door. Finally, the seaweed arms reveal their full mass, and their cargo. They're dragging Conor. They're wrapped around both of his legs and his waist, and they're pulling him toward the window across the room that looks out toward the beach.

Shannon screams. She tries to run away from the mass of seaweed, but there aren't many places she can go, so she hobbles toward Kayleigh, who is still sliding around on the floor as if she's trying to stand up on an oil slick.

"You've got to call someone, Kayleigh!" Shannon screams. She scratches at her arms and legs like she's trying to peel her own flesh off. *"It won't come off! I can't get it off!"*

She turns back toward her husband, who is still lying motionless in the bathroom doorway. His skin has grown even more red, so bright he almost looks radioactive. He's also developed several clusters of juicy-looking blisters, all over his neck and arms. They're huge and yellow, like egg yolks, and Shannon wants to puke, but she holds it together.

The seaweed continues pulling Conor across the room. He tries to scream, but the plant matter has worked its way over his mouth and down his throat too, and all he can do is whimper and choke as tears roll down his cheeks.

Shannon suddenly feels a new sensation on her arms. They itch, but she also feels as if she's being pulled by some unseen force.

"Mom?" Kayleigh says, crying. "What's happening?"

Shannon looks down to the floor and sees her daughter face down in a puddle of something clear and slippery. She's slicked in it too. Is it just water? Or some kind of slime? She can't tell, but it's flecked with hundreds of tiny white dots.

Shannon looks down again at her own arms and sees something beyond unnatural. The sand on her skin, the sand that she can't seem to brush away, is moving now. It's pulling at her. Somehow, each individual grain is tugging at her flesh. She can feel it, can see them stretch the skin away from the bones. They're working together, reaching for the window.

Then Andrew grunts from across the room. He's still unconscious, but it's happening to him too. The yolky blisters covering his bright red skin are pulling at him. One of them bursts, exploding its pus all over him, creating a lubricant to help slide his weight across the floor.

Shannon and Kayleigh both scream. They're unwillingly getting closer and closer to the window, joining up with Conor, with Andrew following close behind. They scream again. Conor tries to join in, not knowing what else to do. Even Andrew is groaning now. His body rolls over to reveal that his eyes and mouth are beet red and swollen shut with massive yellow blisters, which take turns squirting and oozing their liquid all over him.

They scream again and again, and a moment later, the window shatters.

•••••••••••••

Kayleigh wakes up on the beach to the sounds of waves crashing and seagulls squawking. She's groggy, but otherwise feels fine. She's lying on the sand, the sun beating down from above. Conor is there too, lying to her left. He seems to be asleep, and no longer covered in seaweed. She nudges his shoulder, then turns to her right, where both of her parents are. They seem fine too, even if they're not conscious. Her mother looks the same as she always has, her skin free of the sandy coating she had in the room. And her father no longer appears to be suffering the effects of sunburn. He's perfectly tan, just like he always has been.

Just as Kayleigh reaches toward her mom, both of her parents stir and wake. Their eyes crack open but remain as slits defending against the brightness of the sun above.

"Mom, are you okay? Dad?"

"Yeah, I think so," Shannon says, her voice ragged and sleepy.

"I had a terrible dream. I—"

But the looks on her parents' faces tell Kayleigh all she needs to know. It wasn't a dream.

She turns toward Conor, who has woken and started to sit up. He tries to speak, but gags instead. Then he coughs, dislodging something into his mouth. He leans further forward, now sitting upright, and extracts a small wad of slimy green-black seaweed from between his teeth.

Kayleigh's eyes go wide, but just as suddenly, something thuds behind her. She turns, as do the rest of her family, to find a volleyball in the sand. A shirtless man in his late twenties approaches with an apologetic hand raised. He wears a baseball cap on backwards, and he's slicked with sweat from an afternoon of exercise in the sun.

"Close one. Sorry about that," he says. He bends down to pick up the ball before Kayleigh can turn around to get it for him.

"No problem," she says.

"Hey, uh, first day here, right?" the man says. He looks around to all four members of the family, all of whom are still wearing looks of befuddlement. "I saw you try to leave earlier."

"Yeah, we—" says Andrew.

"I know you're probably pretty confused right now. I had a similar reaction when I first got here," the man says. "But, uh, you can't."

"Can't? Can't what?" Shannon asks, her voice now slightly clearer.

"Leave," the man says.

"Staaaaaaaaaay." Kayleigh hears the voice again, just as she had earlier. It's a whisper on the ocean breeze, something she's still not entirely sure she's hearing correctly.

She focuses, attempting to block everything else out for a moment, and tries to listen to the wind. And she hears it again. *"Staaaaaay."* There's no mistaking it this time. It takes a minute, but each time she hears the voice, it becomes more and more clear. *"Musssst staaaaay."*

"Wait, what are you saying?" Andrew asks the stranger. "How long have you been here?"

"I don't even know, to be honest. But there are worse places to spend forever. There's food, and showers, and you really can't beat the weather. It's the same every day. And the nights are just as nice. We all usually gather for the sunset and do a whole bonfire thing."

Shannon's jaw drops. "You mean we're stuck—"

"Yeah. It's...well, we don't really know what it is. But this place, it lures people in. At least, we think it's this place. It might be the seagulls for all we know. But whatever it is, it makes you stay here, and it feeds off your energy, somehow. I don't really get it. I just know nobody ever leaves."

Shannon and Andrew have no further response. Along with Kayleigh and Conor, they're terrified by what they've just been through, and what they're hearing now.

"Anyway, we all try to make the best of it. Like I said, it could be much worse."

There's a moment of silence between them all. The sound of the water creeps in from the edges.

"Oh, uh, you see those cabanas down that way?" The man extends his arm and points to his left. "Pretty much anything you need, you can get down there. Sunblock, drinks, first aid supplies, whatever. They even have some of those old-fashioned postcards with the big letters that say 'Greetings from Trammel Beach' on them. Not that you can mail them from here, but it's a cute touch."

The man looks up as a sudden shadow starts sliding down the top of his head.

"Hey, speaking of which, you're gonna want to back up this way about ten or fifteen feet. It's Picture Day. At least that's what we call it. Happens once every few months around this time of day."

Kayleigh is the first to turn back and look up to see what's blocking the sun. She can't believe her eyes.

"Here, I'll help you with your stuff," the man says, and they gather their things and move as quickly as they can.

Once they've relocated, the four of them, along with their new acquaintance, gaze up at the giant forms descending from the sky as their faces temporarily darken in shadow. There are twelve shapes, all separate, but moving together as if interlocked—twelve enormous bold letters, each stroke thick, with rounded corners. Kayleigh can't tell what they're made of—if they're inflated balloons or concrete being lowered by some unseen crane. Each letter has thick orange sides, but their facades display a dozen different scenes from other areas of the beach, all playing out live like oddly-shaped video screens.

Finally, the gigantic words TRAMMEL BEACH settle on the sand with a deep thud, and the words "Greetings from", in smaller script, yellow like the blazing sun, follow just behind and rest atop them.

"Smile, everyone!" the man calls out, and the rest of the beachgoers begin to cheer. Even the seagulls floating above screech, in what seems like celebration. The man leans in toward Kayleigh and her family. "Seriously, try to look like you're having a blast."

Kayleigh turns toward her parents, and then to Conor. They all have wide eyes and expressions of terror on their faces. But somehow, very quickly, their faces change. Up close, the expressions look forced, but from a distance, no one would be able to tell the difference. They look so happy. Like they're having the vacation of their lives. Like they could stay here forever.

•••••••••••••

The bell over the door of the gift shop jingles.

"Hi there. Do you sell sunblock?"

"Sure do, but it's not the highest protection."

"Oh, that's okay. Whatever you've got is just fine."

"Here you are, sir."

"How about postcards?"

"You bet. In fact, we just got some new ones in. 'Greetings from Trammel Beach'. Have you been down to the water yet?"

"No, not yet, but that's where we're headed today. Figured we'd send a few postcards first. Ya know, make our friends jealous."

"Sounds good. We hope your friends come for a visit someday too."

COLD HANDS

My husband shudders at my touch. He jerks away from me the moment I establish any contact with him. He says my hands are too cold.

Sitting beside him, I place my fingers on the back of his hand, but he pulls away. I touch his back, just below the neck, and he flinches. I brush my hand past his elbow and he jolts, a violent motion that sends a momentary wave of panic through me.

Sometimes he is more emphatic. He gets loud. He berates me. Sometimes he leaves bruises. But I still love him. And I have no one else.

Our home is quite secluded, out here in the country. I have no other family, and it's rare for me to see friends since we moved away from where I spent my childhood. But it's still quite nice, and quiet most of the time.

He tells me again how cold my hands are. I remind him of the old saying, but he doesn't want to hear it. He goes about his business and we don't speak again until "goodnight". I lie awake in bed into the wee hours, one hand in the other, not even feeling the coldness he despises so much, and eventually fall asleep for a few hours.

Most nights go like this.

Autumn is here, and the sun is down earlier than it used to be. The nights are chilly, and my husband builds fires with regularity.

One evening he is crouched in front of our fireplace. Not realizing the work is nearly done, I step up alongside him and ask if he needs any assistance. When he doesn't respond, I place a hand on his shoulder to get his attention. He is surprised by my touch, and tips forward, nearly falling into the flames.

He regains his balance quickly and stands, screaming vile things at me. He swipes at me like a wild beast, but misses, and I am suddenly thankful he drank too much wine with dinner. He huffs and stares at me with angry eyes, and everything within me tenses, but then he gives up the moment and staggers away.

Our home is not very large, but I still don't see him again that night. Our time apart, I hope, will give his temper time to dissipate.

Quietly, I pull a chair forward and sit alone before the crackling fire for some time, rubbing my hands together in the light. They don't feel any warmer to me, although I never thought they were cold to begin with.

When I wake in the chair the next morning, my

husband has already left. He has business in the city, and I don't expect him home until quite late.

I go about my own work at home. There is laundry to do, food to prepare, and several pieces of correspondence I have been putting off.

At some point I notice how dirty my hands have become. They are gray with filth, from fingertip to wrist, as if they had been smeared with the burned end of a cork. I certainly can't prepare a meal this way.

I brush my palms together a few times to clear some of the crud away. Then I rub the back of one hand with the thumb of the other. But the dirt won't budge.

What is this? I think to myself, nearly saying it out loud. *Soot from last night's fire? Did I sit by the fireplace for so long that I took on the quality of charred wood? Or is it simply grime from my cleaning? Was there something mixed in with the clothes I had started to launder?*

I run my hands under water, lathering them with soap, but still the gray color won't go away. Even stranger, the discoloration appears to end in a hard line on both wrists. It's as if I am wearing gray gloves on both hands. How odd this is.

I decide to get back to work. If I don't, there won't be any meal waiting for my husband when he returns from a long day of work and travel, and I certainly don't want to upset him. I have a pair of cotton gloves I can wear while preparing the food. They're a bit cumbersome, but I'd rather we didn't get sick from whatever it is I've amassed on my hands.

That night, my husband comes home even later than expected. He is grumpy, but does not seem as overtly angry as he was when we parted ways last night. We eat by candlelight but barely speak. I want to tell him about the gray filth I can't seem to wash off my hands, and I want to hear how his business in the city went, but his mood is foul. He doesn't notice my gloves, or at least doesn't ask about them. Perhaps he assumes I am making an effort to warm them up for his benefit.

The weather has improved significantly, and there's no need for a fire.

My husband eats quickly, shoveling food into his mouth, then goes straight to bed. I am left to clean things up after our meal. I spend extra time scrubbing my hands with a hard-bristled brush, expecting them to turn red instead of gray, but to no avail.

I crawl into bed beside my husband several hours later. He is snoring and muttering something between breaths. I press his shoulder, in an attempt to roll him onto his side, to stop his snoring. Even in his sleep, he jerks violently away from my touch and swats at me lazily, shouting the word "cold" in an annoyed, if slurred, tone.

After an hour or so passes, I decide I am not tired after all, and get back out of bed. I step into the next room, light a candle, and pore over our collection of books.

I run a finger along the spines of the various hardcover volumes on the shelf. None of them recoil from my touch. Even in the dim light I can see the discoloration of my hands, and the lines on my wrists where the color changes back to my normal tone. It's as if a shadow has been cast on my hands—a shadow that moves with them wherever they go.

I decide on something to read and tug at the top of the book's spine, trying to pull it forward. It tips slightly, but seems to be stuck to its neighbors. We have overstuffed our shelves.

I continue to pull at the chosen volume, while using a second hand to push some of the other books aside.

And in the stillness of the night, I hear the soft sound of flesh separating. It is not a tearing sound. It is not violent. It is like a gentle bite into an overripe peach.

And my hands—both of them—fall to the floor. *Th-thud.*

I gasp and raise my wrists up to my face, unable to believe what has just happened.

My hands land on their backs, then quiver and flop onto their palms like a pair of fish on dry land. Even in the low light, I can see they're very much alive. They look like strange little hairless gray beasts. Then they skitter away into the shadows, and I gasp again.

After an inspection of my wrists—which don't bleed, but simply terminate—I tuck them under opposite arms. I tiptoe around the room searching for my hands, terrified I might wake my husband in the next room. Despite what is happening, that's the last thing I want now. I hear the hands shuffle from time to time, but there isn't enough light to track them down. They seem to know to stay in the shadows.

Eventually I go back to bed, and with some difficulty, I manage to get the covers up over my shoulders without disturbing my husband. I don't sleep much, and find myself repeatedly startled by the tiniest of sounds.

When I wake the next morning, he has already left for the day. Once again he has business in the city, and is due home late. This gives me time to search for my hands.

Where have the little gray creatures gone?, I wonder. I call to them. I search room to room. I look in corners and in cabinets, beneath chairs, behind curtains. I cannot find them anywhere. Occasionally I'll hear a noise, and wonder if it's them, or just the wind outside the window.

I struggle through the day, but manage without my hands. I'm able to make the evening's meal, although it takes twice as long and the results look haphazard, to say the least.

I don't want to trouble my husband about the situation. He's got enough to worry about with his business dealings, and he never liked my cold hands anyway. For all I know, he'd take great delight in the fact that they've gone missing. And even if they were found, he might simply discard them with a laugh. *What a thought!*

I choose to avoid all of this and manage, with some difficulty, to eat my dinner alone, as quickly as I can. I am in bed, tucked well beneath the covers, before my husband returns from the city.

He checks on me, asking if I am ill. I tell him I am just exhausted and need time to rest. I let him know his dinner is keeping warm in the oven. He grunts in response, then goes off to eat and relax for a while, before coming to bed himself several hours later. I am still awake, but pretend to be asleep.

He reeks of wine and staleness. He climbs into the bed and sidles very close to me, planting sloppy kisses upon my neck and shoulder, and soon he is attempting to climb atop me. I manage to fend him off with a strategic turn of my hips and a soft jab of my elbow. He gives up sooner than I expect and begins snoring softly within moments, and suddenly I am at least momentarily thankful for his drinking habit.

Once his breathing deepens even further, I leave the

room, and continue the search for my hands. I wonder if they might be more active after dark. The way they scurried off on their own the night before, they reminded me of the sort of beasties that mill about in the hours after the sun has gone down.

The house is chilly. My husband must not have bothered with a fire. Perhaps he was just too tired after a long day.

Several times I hear little noises, but they are just as likely to be the settling of the house as they are to be a pair of disembodied hands.

I try to think what I would do if I was them. *Where would I go? Would I need sustenance? How would I go about gaining it?*

I sit and think. I pull a quilt over my body with my wrists, and throw it past my shoulders to keep it in place.

How frigid my hands must be now! If they were cold before, imagine what they must be like without a body to keep them warm!

Lost in thought, and without realizing it, I fall asleep upright in the chair.

Hours later, the sun creeps through the windows. I am groggy upon waking, but immediately sense that something isn't right. My husband was scheduled to go into the city for a third and final day of business, but I can see that his coat and shoes are still here. I wonder what could be the matter.

Perhaps he drank too much wine. Or perhaps he fell more seriously ill during the night and is unable to get out of bed. I fear he'll be angry with me for not being in the room to care for him.

I stand and wrap the quilt around my body like a cape, tucking my wrists inside the edges, so as not to give away my malady. I go to the bedroom, dreading what mood I might find him in, and find the bed a shambles. He is lying still among the disheveled covers.

I say his name, but he does not respond. He doesn't move. I repeat his name, louder, but still nothing. If I had my hands, I would be sure to touch his shoulder, to get some reaction, even if it is a violent one.

When I get closer, I see why he doesn't respond. The sheets are stained dark and wet, and my husband's chest has been torn apart, as if by wild animals. Past the shredded flesh, I can see exactly what happened, though I can't imagine why I wouldn't have woken up during the commotion, even from my place in the other room. There, beneath the opening in his chest, beyond his shattered breastbone and broken ribs, lay my cold, gray hands, nestled along either side of his unmoving but still warm heart.

THE TRUNK

"You don't wanna know what's in this trunk," the man said.

He was talking to no one in particular, everyone and anyone who walked by. He was very tall, and wore an overcoat with hands buried in the pockets. He had long, stringy hair, over which he wore a hat—one with a wide brim which kept most of his face in shadow.

He was leaning up against the side of a car—something at least four decades old, maybe five—at the back end, alongside the trunk to which he'd been referring. He had an accent, which was vaguely Southern, but difficult to place.

"I'm telling ya," he said, "You really don't wanna know what's in this trunk."

For the most part, the occasional passersby gave him little notice, if any at all. They had things to do and places to be, and simply weren't interested in whatever weird reverse psychology game this stranger was playing, or, more likely, whatever he might be attempting to sell.

He bent a knee and propped the heel of one foot on the side of the car, near the back fender, kicking loose a bit of the dust that had accumulated on its ancient paint job. It was a dry, rusty sort of day, with the sun baking the moisture out of everything.

The car was parked perpendicular to the sidewalk, despite the fact that the lines painted on the pavement were angled. It took up the majority of two spots.

"No-sir-ee," he said, louder than before. "You definitely do not want to know what is in this trunk." This time, his head was turned so far to the right, he was practically speaking over his shoulder. He scanned the other side of the street, watching people enter and exit the shops, going about their business without paying him any mind. He hoped he wouldn't have to spend too much longer in this sun.

"What's in the trunk?"

The stranger, startled, whipped his head back around to discover a plump man in a tan suit standing to his left. He wore an enormous belt buckle and had very thin hair on the sides of his head, which he had combed delicately over the barren space on top.

The stranger tried to hide his surprise. He pulled a pack of cigarettes from one of his coat pockets and brought one to his face, along with a lighter, which he instantly sparked to flame. Somehow, the light didn't affect the shadow over his face at all.

"Excuse me. What's—"

"Oh, you don't want to know," the stranger said, exhaling smoke.

The man with the buckle kicked at a small mound of dirt that had been baked onto the sidewalk, and tipped his head back.

"Oh yeah?" he said.

The stranger nodded. "That's what I said."

"Well, friend, ya mind if I take a look anyway?"

"That's up to you," the stranger said. "But I don't think it's something you really want to do."

The man with the buckle stepped forward, paused, and gave a look to the stranger, trying to find his eyes beneath the brim of his hat.

The stranger took his foot off the side of the car and stood straight, turning to face the man with the buckle. He reached for one of his inside pockets and extracted a key, then set it down on top of the trunk with a *clink*.

The man with the buckle paused again, then took another step forward and gently picked the key up. He inserted it into the lock slowly, almost cautiously, before giving it a turn. The lid popped, which startled him even though he expected it, and the man let it rise as a bit of dust puffed off the surface and out from within. He waved a hand in front of his face to clear the air and stifled a cough, glancing over at the stranger one more time before looking in.

The trunk was deep, and like the stranger's face, it somehow seemed to absorb light. The man with the buckle had to lean down to see what was to be seen. He squinted and held a hand over his eyes like a visor, hoping it would help his vision adjust, because he was just barely able to make out what was inside.

"What is that?" he asked. "A footlocker?"

The box took up almost all the available space inside the trunk. He wondered how it even fit. It was darkly colored, either navy blue or black, with silver decorative elements on all its edges and corners. In the front was a large buckle, not unlike the one on his belt, secured with a small lock of its own.

"Sure, a footlocker," the stranger replied. He took a long drag from his cigarette and held it, then exhaled a column of white smoke. "Some might call it a trunk."

The man with the buckle chuckled.

"You serious?" he sputtered. "You're out here tellin' people, 'You don't wanna know what's in this trunk,' and it's just another trunk? Ha! Ya damn weirdo!"

The stranger smiled and took yet another puff while the man with the buckle continued to laugh.

"Yeah, well, you sure don't wanna know what's in that trunk," the stranger said.

"You're a riot!" the man with the buckle exclaimed, laughing at the absurdity of the situation. He grabbed the sides of his belt-line and hoisted his pants up an inch, then smacked his hands together. "Well, alright, let's see what we got here!"

"No, no," the stranger said. "I think you ought to reconsider. I really don't believe you want to know what's in that trunk."

"Oh you don't bel—? Well, listen here, friend. I'm the mayor of this here town, and if I want to examine the contents of an illegally parked automobile sittin' right outside my office, then I've got that right. And if you don't believe me for some reason, I can have the sheriff here in a matter of minutes."

The stranger didn't respond with words. He simply produced another, smaller key from one of his coat pockets and offered it to the mayor, who glared at the shadow underneath the stranger's hat.

"I'll say it again," said the stranger. "I don't think you want to know what's in that trunk. But, of course, I can't stop you from looking."

The mayor said nothing, but grabbed the key and leaned into the back of the car, to unlock the trunk inside the trunk. He had to wiggle the key to make it work, but finally the lock gave. When he raised the hinged lid of the footlocker, he was disgusted to find the bloodied, severed trunk of an elephant.

The mayor pulled back quickly, bringing a hand to his face in an effort to keep too much of the stench from entering his nostrils. He coughed, and made grunting sounds of disbelief.

"Told ya," the stranger said, laughing softly to himself.

The trunk inside the trunk inside the trunk was gray, its flesh rough and wrinkled except at one end, where the neutral tone gave way to jagged shreds of pink and red. The bottom of the footlocker was wet with gore. It all stank, rotting in the heat.

"Just what in the hell is going on here?!" the mayor exclaimed, having regained his composure. He pulled a handkerchief out of his pocket and wiped around his mouth, then across his forehead. He slammed the lid of the car's trunk down, but it didn't catch; instead, it just bounced back open. He didn't make a second attempt.

"I told you ya didn't wanna know what was in that trunk," the stranger repeated. "People don't listen."

"That's it," the mayor said. "I've had about enough of this. We're gonna have a talk with the sheriff."

"Alright," the stranger said. "But can I say just one more thing before we do?" He took one last pull from his cigarette while waiting for a response, but the mayor offered none. The stranger exhaled, then licked his lips and dropped the butt to the ground, where he used a toe to grind it into the pavement. "You definitely, absolutely, positively—no question—do *not* want to know what's inside that trunk."

The mayor cocked his head to one side as a look of incredulity washed over his face.

"Are you goddamned crazy?" he said after a beat, as he moved his eyes from the stranger's shadowy face to the trunk inside the trunk inside the trunk. "Just what the hell do you take me for?"

Then, as if right on cue, the elephant trunk burst open, turning itself inside out, and spilled forth a mushy mass of yellow sludge, like mashed potatoes and butter. The smell was unbearable, but the mayor didn't have a chance to pull away. The expanding mound of rot inside the footlocker expelled a cloud of fine particles directly into his face, knocking him back a step before doubling him over in a fit of uncontrollable coughing, which soon dropped him to his knees.

The mayor hacked and wheezed, unable to breathe, while the stranger stood calmly off to the side. Tears began to roll down the mayor's cheeks as he struggled to catch his breath. He placed a hand on the sidewalk and tried to push himself back up to his feet, but he was hit with another wave of coughing and stayed where he was.

The pale yellow mush that the elephant trunk had become took over the entire inside of the car trunk now. It dissolved the footlocker entirely. Then, from within the rotten mass, dozens of small, hard-shelled, crab-like things emerged. They skittered around the inside of the storage space and quickly moved to line the perimeter, clicking their claws with fervent anticipation.

The stranger glanced around to make sure there were few, if any, witnesses, then stepped over to the mayor. He picked him up by the back of his belt with one hand and tossed him, almost effortlessly, into the trunk of the car like a piece of empty luggage. In the process, his belt buckle popped off and hit the ground with a clatter. The stranger kicked it to the curb.

The crab-things went to work immediately, razoring and mincing the mayor into pulp in a matter of seconds. The pale mush enveloped and absorbed him, before retracting into some unseen depth of the car's inner workings.

The vehicle shuddered as the ignition started, kicking loose every bit of dust its exterior had accumulated. Suddenly the painted surface looked fresher, shinier, somehow newer. The engine rumbled, as if clearing its throat.

"I tried to tell him," the stranger said softly. Then he slammed the trunk closed and climbed into the driver's seat. And the car drove off to the next dusty town.

GOURDS

What the fuck is this? Marshall thought. He nearly said it out loud.

He'd just walked through the door, hadn't even had the chance to call out "Honey, I'm home", when he noticed the strange looking objects on the foyer table.

There were three of them, each slightly different. One looked vaguely like a small watermelon, though it clearly wasn't.

The one in the middle looked diseased. He stepped closer and sniffed, but didn't detect any rot. Marshall picked the thing up, then held it aloft to regard its odd form, its bumps and bubbles, the streaks of orange, yellow, and green that colored it. It was shaped more or less like an eggplant, but its color and warts made him think eggplant-plus-pumpkin-plus-cottage-cheese, an unholy union that had somehow birthed a deformed, demonic vegetable.

Is that what these were? Vegetables? And if so, why would Linda have put them in the foyer instead of the kitchen?

"What the fuck?" This time he did say it out loud, though it was under his breath.

He turned the thing in his hands and rubbed his fingers over the myriad bumps on its surface. They were fleshy, but had a glossy finish, almost as if the thing had been shellacked. The look and feel of it unnerved him.

He set it down and picked up the last of the trio. It was smoother to the touch and had a bulbous base, which tapered into a long, slightly curled, almost phallic shape. *Some sort of weird root vegetable, perhaps?*

"Hey," Linda said, entering the room. "What do you think?"

Marshall flinched, startled by his wife's entrance. He set the vegetable, or whatever it was, back down on the table.

He flashed her a look that was more of a question.

"They're gourds," Linda said. But the expression on Marshall's face told her the word wasn't registering. "Like squash. It's Fall. I figured we could get in the spirit."

"Wait…so…*this is dinner?*"

"No, silly. They're just decorations. I thought they looked nice, and they're, you know, classier than pumpkins. Plus, no need to carve them."

Marshall looked at his wife, looked at the gourds, then looked at his wife again. He shrugged.

"Okay."

Then he loosened his tie and motioned toward the kitchen with his head. He was ready to eat.

•••••••••••

Marshall couldn't stop thinking about the gourds.

He didn't hear a word his wife said all through their meal together. He assumed she talked about her workday. That's how it usually went. Normally he was so exhausted by his own workday that he was happy to just sit and listen while he ate.

But this time, he wasn't able to focus on anything she was saying. His mind kept wandering to those things on the table in the other room. They were very strange looking, and yet there was something alluring about them. He couldn't quite nail it down.

After dinner, he washed the dishes while Linda called her mother. They reconvened in front of the TV an hour later and watched half a movie. Marshall didn't even know what it was. His mind was elsewhere, with those oddly-shaped things in the foyer.

In particular, he was fixated on the one with the "diseased" look, the one with the blistered surface. It reminded him of the oatmeal raisin cookies his mom used to make when he was a kid, and how they used to laugh at how imperfect they looked with their lumps.

"Go to bed, honey," Linda said.

Marshall hadn't realized he had been nodding off, his eyelids dropping like shades and his head tipping backward against the couch cushion.

"Come on, Marshall. You're snoring."

•••••••••••

Somehow, Linda had gotten Marshall into the bedroom. He wasn't able to remember the process the next morning; he had only the vaguest recollection of being told he was falling asleep. The next thing he knew, he was waking up to the screeching sound of his alarm, face down on the pillow with one leg hanging off the edge of the mattress.

As the coffee brewed and he got himself prepared to leave for work, he thought of the gourds again, and realized he had dreamt of them all through the night. In the dream, he had been walking around the house in the early morning hours, naked, with the lights out. As he approached the gourds on the table, they began speaking.

Was that right? He couldn't recall seeing any mouths—though it was quite dark in the dream—but he certainly had the impression the gourds had communicated with him somehow. But that's all he could remember.

"You know, if you didn't like them, you could've just said something," Linda remarked, entering the kitchen.

"Huh?"

"What do you mean 'huh'? The gourds. You could've just told me you didn't like them. You know I hate this passive-aggressive bullshit."

"What are you talking about?" Marshall responded. He hadn't been anywhere near the gourds since he walked through the door last night.

Linda left the room. Marshall followed behind her a beat later. She led him to the foyer, where she walked to the table, picked up the object in the middle, and turned around to present it to him.

"This. This is what I'm talking about," she said. She held the bumpy gourd with both of her hands cupped beneath, and Marshall could see exactly what she meant. The thing had been split open, practically turned inside out, all of its seeds and stringy interior bits exposed in a sloppy mess on the table, and now in his wife's hands.

One of the other two gourds had been halved as well. Only the long, curled one seemingly remained intact.

"I..."

"This is really mean, Marshall. It's not like they're expensive or anything. It's just...why? I would've gotten rid of them, or at least put them somewhere else."

"Linda, I don't know what happened. I didn't do this."

"Yeah, well, Buster died six months ago, so I don't think it was him. Plus, he only ever seemed interested in squirrels."

"I'm sorry, honey. I don't know what to tell you," he said. "But I'm late. I need to run. We can talk later."

•••••••••••••

The rest of Marshall's morning was filled with irritated coworkers and phone calls he hadn't been looking forward to. Every Thursday was like this lately, but it all seemed to hit a little harder this week—probably because of the altercation he and Linda had had just before he left.

The new guy in the Billing department was screwing things up left and right. *So why didn't he have to call the clients whose accounts he had double-billed?* Somehow the responsibility had fallen to Marshall, on top of all the other work he was behind on.

By 11:30, he was ready for lunch, and in need of

some fresh air anyway, so he put his computer to sleep and hit the restroom to wash his hands.

That's when he noticed the bumps. His head was throbbing, and he was feeling warm, so after rinsing off, he placed his cool, wet palms against his face for a bit of relief. When he moved his fingers up to massage his temples, he felt something just inside the edges of his hairline. Several small lumps, like hard blisters or mosquito bites. Pressing against them hurt more than it relieved his pain, though, so he didn't linger.

Glancing in the mirror, he was able to spread his hair and see them. There were several spots on each side of his head, easily hidden within his prematurely graying temples. The largest of them was not quite the size of a penny, but most were significantly smaller.

He wasn't sure what it meant, but the discovery of the spots killed his appetite, and he decided to skip lunch and instead go right back to his desk. He didn't want to think about a dermatologist appointment on top of everything else he had to do, so he tried to occupy his mind with work as best he could.

The rest of the day was a blur. He thought of the gourds constantly, despite trying to focus on his job. By the end of the day, he was so wrapped up in the complexities of the company's latest major billing error that he had no idea how much work he had actually gotten done.

•••••••••••

Marshall had no memory of his journey home. It was as if he had blinked at work and then stepped through the front door at home upon reopening his eyes.

The house was quiet. Linda typically got home an hour or so before Marshall, but occasionally she got stuck at work late. She usually gave him a heads up when that happened, but he hadn't heard anything tonight. No matter, he thought. His head was still pounding, and he thought maybe he'd just go straight to bed anyway.

The gourds were gone. It took him a moment to notice, but once he did, he felt a wave of sadness crash over him. He had no memory of splitting them open as Linda had accused, but he was upset that she was upset. *Maybe he had done it in his sleep?* He'd had that dream he was roaming the house in the middle of the night. Maybe it wasn't actually a dream. *Had he been sleepwalking?*

Marshall gave his forehead a squeeze, then combed his hand through his hair and noticed more bumps on his scalp. They trailed down the back of his head now, and behind his collar. There had to be thirty or forty of them— far more than there had been earlier. He wondered what could have caused them, and if they might simply go away on their own in a few days.

Suddenly everything seemed far too bright. He made his way to the bedroom and crashed onto the bed.

•••••••••••

"Marshall…"

He woke up at 2am to find the house completely dark and perfectly still. He was alone in bed. Everything felt stiff. He ached all over.

He twisted from his face-down position to his side,

then folded himself upright and sat for a moment. After a few breaths he felt the nausea.

"*Marshall...*"

The voice was a whisper, and it didn't belong to Linda. Marshall wondered where she was. It wasn't normal for her to be up so late. Was she really that mad at him that she decided to sleep in another room?

He reeled in his urge to vomit and got up to find her. He checked the guest room first, but the bed in there remained untouched. The living room couch was empty. The kitchen too was unoccupied. Room by room he searched, but no Linda. *Where could she be? Maybe she decided to spend the night at her parents'?* She had done that a few times in the past, but she had always told him well ahead of time. *This gourd thing couldn't have made her that upset, could it?*

He considered calling his in-laws, but looked at the clock again and decided against it.

Then came the voice again, whispering his name in the darkness.

And right after, a fresh wave of nausea.

Marshall raced down the hall and fell through the bathroom door to his knees just in time. He managed to brace himself with one hand while lifting the toilet seat with the other as his body lurched.

But whatever he was about to puke up was stuck.

He heaved and strained, his body operating on its own, doing what it needed to do to work out the offending material.

He felt his throat stretch beyond what he thought possible. He even touched it with one hand to be sure his perception of things was accurate. Sure enough, his neck was swollen, as if a football had been stuffed inside.

"*Marshall...*"

He tried to ignore the voice, but it was difficult. He couldn't tell where it was coming from. It sounded like it was inside his head—his head, which was now throbbing in a way he had never felt before.

"*You know what you must do...*"

He heaved again, at last expelling the object clogging his throat. His jaw made a sickening crack as the thing slid over his tongue and teeth, and out past his lips. It hit the toilet water with a splash but remained buoyant, floating on the surface, turning ever so slightly in the dim illumination of the night light plugged in by the sink.

It was an oblong shape. It looked like a gourd.

It was mostly smooth in appearance, though it had a few bumps at either end. It was yellow-orange with green streaks, and slicked with some sort of yellow slime. The taste in his mouth was foul.

Marshall gasped, then tried to catch his breath as he fell back against the side of the bathtub. He tried to comprehend what was happening. This had to be another dream.

"*No, Marshall,*" the voice said. Marshall flinched, and his eyes shot wide, but there was no one there. "*That wasn't a dream. And neither is this.*"

The voice, he could tell now, was indeed coming from inside his head.

After a brief reprieve, another wave of nausea kicked in. Marshall pressed himself up and rolled along the edge of the tub, spinning until he was looking down into it. His body lurched anew, and he felt his throat clog up and swell. It was happening again.

The process was faster and smoother this time, as he birthed a second gourd through his mouth. This one was a darker green with a few thin yellow stripes, and it hit the bottom of the bathtub with a thud before rolling toward the drain.

Another gourd followed. The third was an elongated shape like the first, but bright orange. The fourth looked more like a piece of zucchini, while the fifth was rounder, like a small yellow beach ball. A few more came after that, but by then Marshall was bordering on unconsciousness, struggling with the pain in his belly, throat, and jaw. His vision blurred.

He draped himself over the edge of the tub, looking down at the eight or nine or ten gourds, all sitting in a pool of yellow bile. They smelled rank, and he could feel heat coming off them.

Marshall reached for the faucet and turned the handle, letting cold water trickle out. He splashed some in the direction of the gourds and pulled cupped handfuls to his mouth. He felt dazed, drained by the whole experience, but he sucked up as much liquid as he could, and it helped to revive him.

"You know what you must do now," the voice repeated. He was sure it was in his head, but he was also reminded of his "dream", where he thought the gourds were speaking.

The footsteps came next. For a moment, in the relative darkness and the confusion of the night, he had trouble determining where they were coming from. Then he recognized the creaking sound of the door that led to the attic slowly opening.

Marshall turned back around, trying to brace himself against the side of the tub and get to his feet. Before he was able to, Linda appeared in the doorway.

Cradled in her arms were half a dozen gourds, all different shapes and colors, all, like Marshall's, slicked with yellow slime, which also stained her sleeves.

Her eyes were dead. Her face held no expression. But even in the low light, Marshall could see the bumps just above her cheekbones.

"Did they tell you?" she asked. "What we have to do now?"

•••••••••••

"John, are you home?" Meredith carried as many grocery bags as she could, but there were plenty more in the car. "I could use a hand!"

Her husband bounded down the steps a moment later and followed her out to the driveway. The hatch was open, and the back was filled wall-to-wall with overstuffed tote bags.

"Getting chilly," John said. He'd been inside all day.

They both filled their hands with as many bag straps as possible, but they'd have to make one more trip, at least.

"Filled all the canvas ones, huh?" John said. "Where's that plastic one from?"

"Oh, funny story," Meredith replied. "Remember Linda and Marshall Wallace?"

"Sure, we met them at the Hendersons' barbecue last summer, right?"

Meredith nodded. "And she was in that book club I went to a few times."

"Oh right," John said. Meredith had never been

much of a reader. He was surprised when she'd joined that group, but less surprised when she gave up on it a few months later.

"Well, I was driving home, and just as I turned onto Elmhurst, I spotted them both. They had a little table set up on the side of the road. Looked like they were selling vegetables or something. So I just randomly decided to stop and say hi. Plus, the market was out of carrots. Can you believe that? How do you run out of carrots?"

John laughed. He didn't like carrots anyway.

"Anyway, we talked for a minute, but they seemed kind of standoffish. Like they didn't really recognize me or something. So I didn't stick around. Turns out they didn't have much for sale anyway."

"Hmm," John said. "I barely remember what we talked to them about at the barbecue, but they seemed friendly enough."

They set their bags down on the kitchen floor. John turned back toward the front door to go collect the last of the groceries.

"Hold on," Meredith said. "So, as I'm trying to leave, they don't even seem interested in saying goodbye, but they give me these. For free." With one hand, she extracted two objects from the plastic shopping bag, and presented them to John.

He eyed them before taking them into his own hands. One was green and smooth, and shaped like a long, curled balloon a clown would fold into a dog at a kid's birthday party, while the other was more egg-shaped, and orange, with a cluster of knobs and lumps that reminded him somewhat of popcorn.

"Okay then. So…we've been gifted gourds?"

Meredith shrugged her shoulders. "Yup. Weird, huh? But I couldn't *not* accept them, right?"

"Oh sure. It's just an odd gift to receive from people we barely know."

"True," Meredith said. "But Fall's here. Maybe they'll look nice by the window."

"Works for me. What do you feel like doing for dinner?"

•••••••••••

The next morning, John woke up and went downstairs to start the coffee. His head hurt, but he was sure the caffeine would help.

As he tried to recall the vaguest notion of a dream he'd had, he scratched the side of his head and noticed a series of small bumps just inside his hairline.

He also noticed the gourds, which appeared to have fallen off the windowsill overnight and cracked open on the floor below.

Then he heard something—a voice, whispering his name. But it wasn't Meredith. She had already left for work.

CLOWN NOSES

Elliott's earmuffs were on so tight, he didn't notice the man in the bright red clown nose talking to him.

The man stepped closer and raised a hand, making a motion to the side of his own head.

"Yes?" Elliott said, pulling the contraption off his left ear. He was already annoyed his bus hadn't arrived. He wasn't in the mood to talk to a stranger.

"I said it's a cold one, huh?" the man repeated. He had a rather jubilant tone to his voice, which Elliott didn't appreciate in this weather. The man was smiling, but it seemed half his face was obscured by the foam sphere he was wearing.

Elliott half-smiled and half-nodded in response.

"So how ya doin', Elliott?" the man asked. "What's it

been, eight years? Ten?"

Suddenly Elliott connected the dots.

"Oh! Hi there, Shelly," he said, his tone somewhat uplifted. He was cold, running late, and didn't particularly enjoy small talk, but he tried not to be rude. "I didn't realize it was you at first. More like twelve, I think."

"Twelve years," Shelly said, aghast. He shook his head. "Time sure does fly, doesn't it?"

Elliott half-smiled again, and half-covered his ear with the earmuff, so he could stay relatively warm but still hear his old college friend.

Shelly exhaled deeply and a column of air turned white. The underside of his clown nose was wet with condensation.

"So, uh, whatcha got there, Shel?" Elliott asked, nodding at him, narrowing his focus to the red foam nose.

"Oh, this?" Shelly said with a chuckle, pointing to the nose. "Heh, well, ya know, it's a funny thing..."

Elliott raised an eyebrow while Shelly took another cold breath before continuing.

"I can see you're no fan of winter," Shelly began again. "I'm the same way. Always thought it was odd how we have hats and gloves and thick winter socks and coats and vests and scarves and snow pants and on and on and on, but nothing to keep our noses nice and toasty, ya know? You got some nice earmuffs there. Makes sense. So, I figured, what about nose muffs?"

Elliott let out a muted laugh. A voice came over the speaker on the corner, announcing that his bus would be there in two minutes. Inside his mind, Elliott cheered.

"Yeah, nose muffs, right?" Shelly continued. "So

right around the same time the idea struck me, I ran into another old friend of mine. Hadn't seen him in eight or ten years either. Turns out he was on tour with the circus. Guy's a clown. Heh, funny thing. In high school the guy's a star athlete—state championship quarterback, MVP pitcher—then he graduates and runs off to join the circus, just like every little kid dreams about at one time or another. Life's funny, ya know?"

Elliott could see his bus in the distance, just two blocks away. It couldn't get there fast enough. He continued to smile and feign interest.

"Anyway, I was standing there shivering, kinda like you are now, and he cracks some joke about how nice and cozy he felt under that bright red clown nose, and that's when I had my eureka moment. I threw a fiver at him and plunked the foam off his nose right then and there. Been wearing one of these ever since!" Shelly slapped Elliott on the shoulder.

"Wow," Elliott said with mock enthusiasm. He took a step toward the street, as the bus approached. A gust of wind barreled through the intersection and Elliott hunched his shoulders.

"Never been happier!" Shelly exclaimed.

"Yeah, that's great," Elliott said. "Really something. Hey, good to see you, Shelly."

"You too, Elliott! Twelve years, huh? Can't believe how time flies." Shelly looked down at the sidewalk for a second, shaking his head. "Hey, let's grab a drink some—"

But Elliott had already boarded the bus. The doors closed as Shelly looked up and frowned.

•••••••••••

Elliott was sick in bed for the next three days. When he ran out of tissues, he blew his nose into strips of toilet paper. Then paper towels. Then washcloths. Then old socks.

On the fourth day, he finally felt well enough to go back out into the world. He wasn't sure if he would make it all the way to work, but he was going to try. At the very least, he had to go buy some more tissues.

He stood, shivering, waiting for the bus. His earmuffs were in place, and his arms were crossed. Winter was really getting into its groove.

"Heyyyy! There he is!" announced Shelly. "I was starting to worry about you, old friend."

"Oh, hi, Shel. Yeah, I've pretty much sick in bed since I last saw you."

"Yeah, you don't look so hot...heh, so to speak," Shelly said with a chuckle as he stepped closer. "By the way, I got you something."

Shelly reached a closed fist toward Elliott, paused for effect, then opened his hand to reveal a globe of bright red foam.

Elliott laughed.

"Thanks," he said. "I'm good."

"No, no, it's fine," Shelly said.

"I've been sick, though," countered Elliott. "I wouldn't want to—"

"That's exactly why you need one of these," Shelly said. "Don't worry—it's brand new. Never worn. I wouldn't give ya any old leftovers, my friend, and I'm not expecting it back."

"Well, thanks. What do I owe you?"

"Owe me? Nothing! It's a gift!" Shelly said. "Don't

you worry about a thing. Besides, I get a deal on these now through that friend of mine."

"Thanks again, Shelly." Elliott was about to place the clown nose over his own, but noticed his bus approaching, so he tucked it into his pocket instead. "Take care."

Shelly, wearing his own clown nose, waved to Elliott from the street, and remained standing there until the bus had pulled away.

On the bus, Elliott pulled the foam nose from his pocket and gave it a squeeze. Looking around the bus, he noticed two other people wearing them.

After purchasing two boxes of tissues and a to-go cup of vegetable barley soup, Elliott made his way to work and spent half the day there, before giving up and heading back home to bed. He hoped another full night's rest would do the trick.

•••••••••••

Elliott woke the next morning to find that the temperature had dropped another five degrees. Peeking through the window, he saw a thin dusting of snow had fallen overnight.

He took a long, hot shower, bundled himself up, and made his way to the bus stop. He had the clown nose in his pocket.

When he arrived, sure enough, Shelly was there, dressed in his thick overcoat, gloves, scarf, hat, and bright red clown nose. Three other people waiting for their buses wore clown noses too. Elliott slipped his on before Shelly spotted him.

"Hey friend," Shelly said. "You're looking a bit better today. How's that foam treating you? Nice and toasty?"

"It's great, actually," Elliott said. He wasn't lying. "And it looks like this is catching on, huh?" Elliott motioned to the others assembled on the sidewalk.

"See?" Shelly said. "You probably thought I was crazy, but a good idea's a good idea, right?"

Elliott's bus arrived. Caught by surprise, he nearly didn't move. But Shelly nodded his head toward the vehicle, and Elliott sprang back to life. They said their goodbyes quickly, and Elliott boarded.

By his estimation, at least two-thirds of the people on the bus were wearing clown noses. It was a full-blown fad. It made sense, too. Elliott's nose was warm like he had never experienced in winter before. Sure, everyone looked a little silly, but who cared about that, especially when so many other people were doing the same thing.

Just before Elliott arrived at his destination, he heard the hiss of the speaker system being activated.

"Attention, all passengers," a voice announced. It wasn't clear to Elliott whether it was the driver speaking, or a prerecorded message. "New transit schedules for all lines begin next week. In addition, starting Monday, earmuffs will no longer be legal. The continued use, or mere possession of earmuffs, beginning next week, will be subject to steep fines and/or imprisonment. Please plan accordingly and take the necessary legal precautions to stay warm. It's cold out there. Thank you for your attention."

•••••••••••••

The weekend came and went. Elliott spent most of it resting, in an attempt to shore up his health. Temperatures continued to drop, and forecasts predicted one of, if not the coldest winter on record.

Monday morning, Elliott prepared for work as usual, including his clown nose, and made his way to the bus stop. Shelly, and nearly everyone else waiting, wore a clown nose.

"Elliott!" Shelly hissed. It was clear his instinct was to scream, but he stifled it. "What are you doing, man?!"

"Wh—What do you mean?" Elliott responded, dumbfounded. His recent encounters with Shelly had been nothing if not jolly. He was surprised to see him upset. Thinking back to the days of twelve years prior, he couldn't ever remember Shelly raising his voice or getting angry at anything or anyone.

"Your earmuffs!" Shelly said. He locked eyes with Elliott, then looked sideways as if he was surveilling the place. Shelly stomped toward Elliott and ripped the earmuffs from his head.

"Ow! Hey, what's the idea?"

"*What's the idea?!*" Shelly said. "Are you trying to get locked up?"

"Oh, yeah, there was some kind of joke announcement on the bus the other day..." Elliott said.

Shelly tossed the earmuffs into the trash can on the corner, then brushed his hands together as if he didn't want his fingers tainted with any earmuff germs.

"It's no joke," Shelly said. He looked around the area again, and reached into his pocket. "Here. Take these," he said, pulling a fresh pair of clown noses out.

Elliott took them, but screwed his face in disbelief.

"Look, you're cold, right?" Shelly asked. Elliott nodded. "So put those on your ears."

"What are you talking about, Shel?"

"This is serious, friend," Shelly said. "Police just picked someone up a half hour ago, right here. I saw it all go down. He was wearing earmuffs. They had a little discussion. It got real loud, real fast, and next thing you know, this guy's being thrown in the back of a squad car. Who knows where he is now, but I wouldn't take any chances."

"What the hell is going on?" Elliott said, still not entirely believing what he was hearing. He looked around at the other people waiting for the bus, and not a single one had earmuffs. A few, however, wore clown noses on their ears.

"I don't know, exactly. But this new law seems to be a real thing. Luckily, I got you covered." Shelly motioned toward the clown noses in Elliott's hand. When Elliott didn't react, Shelly grabbed them back, and placed them on Elliott's ears himself. "There. Better?"

Elliott half-nodded. His ears were instantly warmer.

Elliott's bus arrived, and he boarded. He expected a funny look from the bus driver, but she wore three clown noses herself, so Elliott felt a bit better about things. Before long, he was hanging up his coat at work, and slipping the clown noses back into his pocket.

•••••••••••

With each new day, Elliott saw more and more people wearing bright red foam noses on their faces, as well as on their ears. Ridiculous as it looked, it made sense. Sometimes fashion falls by the wayside, in favor of more utilitarian options. You had to keep warm in this weather.

He saw Shelly at the bus stop each weekday, and they stayed friendly, although Elliott never asked why Shelly never boarded the bus.

One day, on his ride into work, Elliott heard the speakers come alive.

"Attention, all passengers," a voice said. "A final reminder. Beginning tomorrow, full-fingered gloves will be outlawed. Again, only fingerless gloves will be permitted starting tomorrow. Failure to comply will, as usual, result in fines and/or imprisonment. Most likely imprisonment. Thank you."

Elliott couldn't believe his foam-covered ears.

The next morning, everyone at the bus stop wore fingerless gloves. And five clown noses on each hand.

As he approached the corner, Elliott could see that Shelly was talking to someone. He handed the guy something, but his back was turned to Elliott, so he couldn't see what.

Elliott had clipped the fingertips off his gloves that morning before leaving the house, and had his hands jammed in his pockets to keep warm.

On the bus, however, an announcement informed everyone that pockets were about to become illegal as well.

The following morning, Elliott handed a crumbled ball of cash to Shelly in exchange for a dozen more clown noses.

●●●●●●●●●●●●

Over the next several weeks, various forms of clothing were declared illegal. There were protests all over town, but each was quickly squashed by authorities. Some people claimed their friends had gone missing. City Hall was closed under the auspices of renovation, not that anyone believed that to be the real reason.

Soon shoes were made illegal. Then hats. Shoulders had to be cut out of all shirts, sweaters, and coats. Knees were mandated to be removed from pants.

People began wearing clown noses on all exposed body parts. Shelly was doing good business, providing Elliott and seemingly all his neighbors with enough red foam to keep them all warm. He even began selling oversize clown noses that fit people's heads and feet and shoulders and knees.

"Things are really getting out of hand," Elliott said to Shelly one morning. Shelly only nodded, focused on the cash in his hands. He'd removed a few of his own clown noses so he could slide the bills from one hand to the other as he counted. It was a frigid morning, and he was trying to count his money as quickly as possible.

Shelly boarded the bus with Elliott that day, which surprised him.

"Gotta replenish my supply," Shelly explained. "Business has really taken off, my friend!"

Everyone on the bus wore bright red clown noses on every part of their bodies.

"That's great," replied Elliott. "Although I gotta say I'm thankful Spring is coming. It's been a brutal winter, and all these new laws have been making everybody crazy."

Shelly smirked, looking past Elliott, and out the window.

There was a massive new tower in the center of town, far taller than any of the other buildings, and it had seemingly gone up overnight. Elliott suddenly noticed how much of the traffic appeared to be cement mixers and flatbed trucks.

It didn't seem to be an office building—instead it was more of a skeletal structure. At the base of the construction, there was an enormous crane with a telescopic arm extending up to the very top of it, gently fitting what had to be the largest clown nose in the entire world onto the tip of the tower's spire.

The foam sphere was enormous. It was, in fact, big enough to block out the sun. A deep shadow was suddenly cast over the entire town, and it instantly began to feel even colder.

"We'll see," Shelly said. "Wouldn't surprise me if we had a chilly Spring too. In fact, I think it might just stay cold for a very, very long time."

ONLY BAD PEOPLE

"Only bad people are buried there."

Johnny heard the comment through the tapestry of voices on the sidewalk, the crowd of pedestrians moving one way or the other, into and out of the various shops that lined this side of Main Street. It was spoken by a child, but having been caught off guard by the words, Johnny wasn't sure if the speaker had been a boy or girl. Not that it mattered. It was the comment itself that struck him.

Was he a bad person?

He didn't like to think of himself that way—*who did?*—but maybe it was true. After all, he had uprooted his life and ultimately come to this town to escape his past mistakes. To start over. People did that sort of thing all the time, landing in new places to restart their lives when things haven't worked out for them.

Johnny sat at one of the tables in front of the cafe, sipping his iced coffee and enjoying the warmth of the day, watching the dueling streams of people make their way up and down the sidewalk. He liked being outdoors, liked the free feeling of the outside air. It was a lovely Saturday, and it was nice to just sit for a few minutes and soak up the atmosphere of his new hometown.

He didn't even know why he had chosen this place. It was just somewhere different. Someplace small and out of the way. Somewhere he could lie low and work on himself for a while.

He hadn't been here very long and didn't know a single person yet. But that was all fine. He needed to focus on getting his head straight anyway. *A clean slate*, he thought.

A few minutes earlier, inside the cafe, he had smiled at a young barista as she handed him his drink. She looked a lot like his daughter, Kelly, if she had been a few years older. He missed her.

But that thought evaporated as soon as he realized the young woman hadn't left any room for cream in his cup. The coffee touched the inside of the plastic lid in such a way that stabbing a straw through the X in the center would surely create a mess. He tried to regain the barista's attention, even as some of the other patrons in line gave disapproving glances in his direction, but with the place as busy as it was, it quickly became evident he wasn't going to succeed.

Johnny moved to the station by the front window where the various creamers and sweeteners were located. He hated the bitter taste of coffee on its own, but with some cream and simple syrup, iced coffee was a magical elixir. He expected to find a small bin, or maybe even a sink, where he could pour out some of his coffee to make room. The cafe he used to frequent had one, but this one didn't seem to. There was a plastic-lined trash can, though, so he made use of that instead.

He felt bad dumping some of his drink into the trash, knowing someone was going to have to empty the bin, and probably end up with coffee soaked hands, or at the very least a trail of liquid that needed to be mopped up, but he didn't feel like he had much of a choice in the moment. The old Johnny wouldn't have given the idea a second thought, so the fact that he felt a twinge of guilt in this instance seemed like progress. It might be happening in baby steps, but he was reinventing himself.

"Only bad people are buried there." The words struck him again as he continued watching the flurry of townspeople passing by his table outside. In the spaces between them, he spied the high cement wall across the street, which ran along the opposite sidewalk. *How strange*, he thought. It seemed like that might have been a good place to put even more businesses.

He had walked on that side of the street earlier without giving the wall a second thought. But from his current vantage point, he was quick to realize how odd it appeared, how out of place it seemed. He could also see the iron rails and spikes that lined the top, which he hadn't noticed before.

He finished his iced coffee and tossed the cup into a trash can on the corner, then crossed the street. There was still a lot about the town he hadn't seen, so he was anxious to explore a bit. He decided to head north until he reached the end of the wall. Maybe then he'd see what was on the other side of it.

Johnny walked for what felt like several city blocks. This was a small town, though, with lots of little streets, so judging the distance wasn't as simple as counting the number of cross streets that broke in on the other side, where all the shops were. Eventually, though, he realized one of the upcoming cross streets continued all the way through Main, which meant he was approaching the end of the wall.

He felt his heart begin to race with anticipation, then realized how silly that was. It was just a wall. *What could it possibly be hiding?*

Reaching the corner led to disappointment. The wall simply turned, continuing around the bend. The second side looked shorter, though. Surely there was an entrance of some sort on this side, or if not, perhaps around the next corner. He continued walking. If nothing else, at least he was getting some exercise. It was good to be outside, good to be seeing some more of his new town.

The second wall was indeed shorter than the distance he had walked along the first. But there was still no indication of its purpose. Finally, when he reached the next corner, he discovered a plaque embedded in the wall—a stone slab with the words HELMUT CEMETERY etched into it, in a classic serif typeface.

So that was it. The walls held a graveyard within. Johnny had always loved cemeteries, particularly older ones, appreciating them for their beauty and serenity. Some people might find them morbid, but Johnny always thought of cemeteries as peaceful places, perfect for meditative walks.

He was intrigued by this one, having never seen a

burial place that was closed off in such a way. Iron fences were typical, but twenty-foot tall cement walls were something else entirely.

He continued walking, hoping he wasn't too far from the entrance.

The third wall was long like the first, making the cemetery a rectangular shape. And, to Johnny's shock, he still hadn't come across any way in. Surely it would be on the fourth wall. And if not, then it had to be on the stretch of the very first wall he hadn't walked along. Either way, it was clear he had chosen to walk in the wrong direction. It was frustrating, but how would he have known? Again, it was good to get some exercise.

He chuckled to himself, suddenly remembering the joke his grandfather used to tell when he was a kid. *"Why are there fences around cemeteries? Because everybody's dying to get in."* He wondered what his grandfather would've thought of this place.

Before long, Johnny was right back where he started, across the street from the cafe. He had completed his circuit around the cemetery but hadn't found any entrance. *Why would it be closed off?* Even if the grounds had been filled to capacity, surely there were still people who would want to visit their departed family members. He couldn't make any sense of it.

There weren't many other people on his side of the street, but he tried asking a few of them what the deal was. In each case, however, the individuals glared at him, as if offended by his asking anything of them. One woman pushing a stroller seemed focused on her child and possibly didn't even hear his inquiry. An older man simply waved a dismissive hand at him and scurried away, clearly not wanting to be bothered by anyone.

What an odd little town, Johnny thought.

Looking up, he noticed gray clouds in the distance and decided he'd had enough walking for the day. Time to head back to his apartment before he got wet. He crossed back over to the side of the street with all the shops, then walked an extra half block or so before pausing and turning back to take another look at the walls.

Having some distance from the cemetery gave him a better perspective. From where he stood now, he was able to see that there seemed to be a hill at one end of the enclosure. He could just barely see it, but there appeared to be a rise just over the top of the wall. He could see a bit of overgrown grass and the tips of what he assumed were tombstones, just a shade lighter than the gray color of the walls surrounding the space.

The clouds above were moving quickly. Johnny felt a drop and decided to race home as quickly as he could.

It rained for several hours, during which Johnny busied himself with organizational tasks inside his new apartment. He'd only moved in a couple weeks earlier, but the place was already a mess. He desperately needed to do laundry and the worn hardwood floors were covered with a scattering of crumbs from two weeks' worth of takeout meals.

The apartment itself was nothing special: a second-floor unit of an old weather-beaten house, with a bedroom, a living room, and a tiny kitchen. It was simple. Utilitarian.

It reminded Johnny a bit of the years just after graduating from college, first living with a roommate, and then striking out on his own in his first solo living experience. That's when he first met Carla, and pretty soon she was staying over most nights and it didn't feel so much like just his space anymore. But that was all fine. They were happy then.

A few years and a few apartments later, Carla surprised him with the pregnancy test she had taken just before he arrived home from work, after which they had gone out to celebrate.

These were good memories. Good times. But things change. People change. One day you wake up and realize your life wasn't what it used to be.

That was all in the past, though. It was time to live in the present and work on himself now. He'd moved on and hit the reset button.

The rain finally stopped after the sun had completely disappeared below the horizon. Johnny ate the remainder of last night's pizza for dinner, then suddenly felt like going out again. He'd spent every night inside since he got to town, so he was due for a night out. He considered going to a bar, but didn't feel like drinking alone, and didn't feel much like making smalltalk with a bartender either.

A movie. That would do it. He hadn't been to see a movie in forever. And as soon as he bought his ticket and some popcorn, he wouldn't need to talk to anyone. He could just sit in the dark and fall into whatever was playing on screen.

He remembered seeing a movie house somewhere just off Main Street. It was one of those older places that probably used to be a burlesque house or Vaudeville theater. He loved old movie houses. He couldn't remember the last time he had been to one.

He arrived not long after making this decision, and

bought a ticket for the next show, which just so happened to be starting in five minutes, from a grumpy box office attendant. He didn't even pay attention to what was screening; he was just happy to be outside his apartment, living life.

He stepped into the lobby and quickly ordered a medium popcorn and large soda. The teenage boy working behind the concession stand filled a paper bag with popcorn, then glazed it with imitation butter, before filling a cup with more ice than soda. He set the items down on the counter and held a hand out for the money owed without saying a word. Johnny wondered why so many people in this town were so unhappy. *Or was it him?* It seemed like everyone he encountered lately was either scowling or dismissive.

He grabbed his snacks and some napkins, and made his way into the theater. The trailers had already started, but there weren't too many other patrons, so he had no trouble finding a seat.

The show turned out to be a repertory screening of an Italian horror film from the 1970's. Although the movie had been dubbed in English, the original Italian title card had not been replaced, nor had it been subtitled, so Johnny had no idea what the film was called. It didn't matter so much, though. He knew that, very often, the titles for these sorts of movies had no bearing on how much of the story you could or couldn't understand.

Johnny wasn't terribly impressed with the film and its bizarre dream logic. During the second half, he began to feel the weight of his eyelids and found his head nodding from time to time. He considered heading home, but the theater seat was surprisingly comfortable and he figured he could make it to the end.

At one point, his head bobbed and he realized two of the other members of the audience were looking back in his direction. *Had he been snoring?* Johnny didn't think he had fallen that deeply into sleep, but anything was possible. He waved an apologetic hand anyway and the concerned filmgoers turned their attention back to the screen.

"Only bad people are buried there."

The line of dialogue, spoken by a child actor, jolted him fully alert. He had completely forgotten about hearing the very same words earlier that afternoon.

He watched as the boy and his mother entered a creepy, fog-drenched graveyard. The action from that point on, despite being filled with a series of mushy-looking zombies, was fairly difficult to follow, especially after having dipped out of consciousness several times, but Johnny made it to the conclusion of the film.

He sat through the end credits, grooving to the prog-rock score, waiting for the rest of the theater to empty, then finally got up to leave himself. As he exited the theater, Johnny realized something he hadn't noticed upon his arrival earlier. The theater was across the street from one of the towering cement walls that enclosed Helmut Cemetery. He shook his head, not understanding how he could have missed that fact earlier.

He went to the nearest intersection and crossed the street, then walked along the wall, which now seemed even more imposing in the yellow light from the lamppost on the corner. He ran his fingers along the wall as he walked, feeling the smooth surface glide against his fingertips.

The walls were angled inward slightly, and he suddenly wondered if it might be possible to scale the wall.

Not that he was interested in trespassing for the thrill of it; he was just curious about why a cemetery seemed to be hidden away from the public.

Something on the wall nicked his finger, stopping Johnny in his tracks. He pulled his hand back and spotted a bead of blood forming on the tip of his middle finger. And in the same moment, he realized he was standing directly in front of the words HELMUT CEMETERY, carved into the slab of stone set into the wall. He had walked right by, and noticed, the very same marker earlier in the day—unless there was more than one. He must have caught his finger on the edge of one of the letters.

Instinctively, he brought his hand to his mouth and sucked the blood away, then realized maybe that wasn't the greatest idea, having just touched a dirty surface. He tasted a hint of the chemical butter from his popcorn in with the iron taste of his blood.

Then he noticed the gate.

It stood to the left of the cemetery's name, forged of black iron, with an elaborate design. It was cloaked somewhat in darkness, falling perfectly into the gap of shadow between the reach of two streetlamps. But Johnny was still dumbfounded. He could see how someone might have trouble finding the entrance at night, but how could he have missed it during the day?

He stepped closer to examine the ironwork. The design seemed purely decorative and non-representational, composed of densely-packed lines, both straight and curved. There were gaps between the lines, but they were small and the graveyard beyond the door was dark, so it was difficult to see within.

Johnny touched the gate and it fell open slowly, the hinges groaning under the weight of the door. He hesitated, then looked down the street in both directions, as if he was doing something he shouldn't. But there was no one in sight. *Cemeteries were meant to be public spaces anyway,* he thought. He stepped through.

The graveyard was dark, but he was able to see enough to navigate his way. There were trees lining the edges of the space, just inside the walls, but the area within the border was open to the sky above. The moon shone big and bright directly above the cemetery; perhaps that, plus the glow of artificial light from the area businesses outside the walls, were enough to illuminate the space to a certain level of visibility.

It was also quite large. Somehow the cemetery seemed even bigger inside the walls than it did from the outside.

The layout of the place was unlike any other cemetery Johnny had ever seen. Sure enough, as he had noticed earlier in the day, there were hills that rose at each of the two far ends, cresting just above the walls. Even in the darkness Johnny could see the tops of the last rows of tombstones at either end, silhouetted against the light from outside the walls. The stones up there must be old, he thought. The tops of them, even from a distance, appeared uneven.

The rows themselves were arranged strangely too, he thought. Normally, in his experience, tombstones were in orderly lines, and evenly spaced. But these were laid out in concentric U-shaped arcs, and more haphazard in their spacing. He didn't see any crosses or decorative carvings. These were just slabs. Some had nicely curved tops, but more of them were jagged, chipped, or broken. They had to be ancient; from where he stood, he wasn't able to detect any names or dates carved into them.

It was an extremely unusual place. But maybe that's why it was, for the most part, closed off. Perhaps the layout was an insurance liability, and maybe everyone buried here was from such a long time ago that no one cared to visit any more.

"Only bad people are buried there." The words returned to his mind once again, in the voice of the child who had spoken them on the street that afternoon. It only now dawned on him how familiar the voice had sounded.

Both hills sloped downward into the center of the cemetery grounds, which sank lower than he would have expected—far lower than street level. It was a deep depression in the earth, with fewer tombstones and hardly any grass. It seemed more like a pit, actually, with the very center in complete darkness.

"They call that the Throat." The voice spoke softly in the darkness, startling Johnny. It was a woman's voice. He spun around to where the sound had come from, in the border of trees. But he couldn't see anyone.

"Don't be frightened," the voice said. Like the child's voice earlier, this woman sounded familiar.

Finally, he located a silhouette in the trees, but could not see any detail.

"Hello," he said. "You gave me a bit of a scare just now."

The shape of the woman stepped forward, and Johnny realized she had a child with her. Neither of them responded to him.

"I didn't realize there was anyone else here," he said,

in another attempt at conversation. But still there was no response.

He turned back to look toward the center of the cemetery again, amazed at how unknowably dark it was there, when he was able to see both of the far ends so much better and more clearly.

"Do you happen to know what the story is with these walls?" As he asked the question, he turned back to the woman and child. They had moved forward a few steps, and their bare feet were now discernible in the moonlight. "Or why it's so hilly here when the rest of the town is so flat?"

But again there was silence. Until, finally, the child spoke:

"Only bad people are buried here."

The pair stepped out from the shadows of the trees, and suddenly Johnny knew why their voices sounded so familiar.

"Kelly?...Carla?" To say he was surprised to see them would be an understatement. He was in shock. His voice wavered. Their presence here wasn't just unlikely. It was an impossibility. And yet there they were, his wife and daughter, standing just a few feet away from him.

"Hi Daddy," Kelly said.

It was so good to hear her voice again. It had only been a couple weeks, but Johnny had feared he had silenced her forever. He sputtered as tears poured down his cheeks.

"Hello, John," Carla echoed. She and Kelly stepped closer. Close enough that Johnny could now see the bruising on Carla's face and the deep gash across her neck. In the moonlight, he could see the dent in the side of Kelly's head too. All wounds he had caused. All mistakes he had been trying to run from. Misjudgments he had made, choices from which he was trying to move on. He wanted to be a better person, but deep down, he knew he was not.

Kelly and Carla walked past him, swiftly now, and moved down the sloped earth, toward the center of the cemetery, the darkest part of the pit.

"Come on, Daddy," Kelly said, turning back toward him, waving one beckoning hand.

His head was buzzing now, the sound of static filling his ears. Tears continued to flow, blotting out his peripheral vision. All he could see now were his wife and daughter. He followed them toward the darkness.

And just before he got there, to the black and sunken patch, the very center of the cemetery that he'd just learned was called the Throat, Kelly and Carla turned back to face him.

"Sorry, Daddy," Kelly said. "But you've been bad."

And with that, Johnny's wife and daughter both evaporated into the darkness, leaving behind only two wisps of black smoke that dissipated as quickly as they had appeared.

Johnny could see nothing else where he stood. It was only when he looked up to the sky that he saw the silhouettes of the two far ends of the cemetery, now moving steadily, arching toward each other over the edges of the walls. In another moment, it seemed, the hills of either end would converge, high above where he stood in the center of the graveyard, sealing him in with whoever else was interred in the dark ground that was slowly beginning to surround him.

The earth beneath his feet was soft, and as if on cue, it began to get softer. He was starting to sink. And he realized then that he hadn't chosen this town. It had chosen him.

The swollen, rounded edges of the hills above looked like a pair of lips to him now, just as the curved rows of grave markers gave the impression of jagged, crooked teeth. He understood now why the center of the cemetery was called the Throat.

He closed his eyes as he sank deeper into it.

THE PENANGGALAN

We fly to Penang, not having any idea what to expect when we get there.

We were supposed to spend our vacation in the Poconos, starting today, at the house Maddie's aunt and uncle own, probably sitting by the river, watching egrets and herons swoop to pinch their meals out of the water. We likely would've taken a hike at least once a day, too, but who knows what else we would've done. We were just trying to get away somewhere, and couldn't afford anything too extravagant.

But then Maddie calls me at work yesterday and tells me about the crazy flight deal she's just found online, and the next thing we know, she's booking it and we're packing for a different trip, and suddenly, now, sixteen hours later, we're traveling halfway around the world for less than it would've cost us to stay in the States all week.

I can't even wrap my head around how fast it all came together. Luckily I already had the vacation time scheduled at work. I don't know how Maddie even found a place for us to stay, but she did.

Now we're sitting on the plane for I don't even know how long. Twelve hours? Fifteen? Twenty? I turn to ask her, but she's already asleep. The wheels haven't even lifted off the runway yet. I wish I could fall asleep the way she does, as quickly as she does. Sometimes I tell her she ought to get checked for narcolepsy.

So I'm sitting here without anything to do, because packing for the trip and securing a ride to the airport was such a whirlwind that I didn't even think to toss a book in my bag, and the TV screen in front of me is broken, and the WiFi on the plane isn't working well enough to load anything on my phone, so I can't even research things to do in the city we'll be touching down in tomorrow morning. I reach into the seat pocket and find the safety card and the in-flight magazine, and I also find this little booklet. It's like a journal with a black leather cover. No title on the front, but the first page inside says it's "A Field Guide to Supernatural Entities in Southeast Asia", and that seems kind of interesting. So I flip through the pages. It's full of ghosts and monsters, all sorts of things from legend and folklore. The kind of stuff I absolutely love. Halfway through, my thumb catches on a page and I'm dumbstruck. The illustration catches me off-guard. It's a beautiful woman—an angelic face with long black hair. But below the neck, she's just a mass of internal organs, hanging there like some disgusting, bloody chandelier. I'm repulsed and attracted at the same time, so I read about who she is.

"The penanggalan is a vampiric creature found in Malaysia. Typically a woman who has practiced malevolent magic, the penanggalan soaks her body in a vat of vinegar so that she can more easily extract her organs from the shell of her outer skin. At night she floats through the air in search of victims. In Indonesia, she is called the leyak, while she is known as the manananggal in the Philippines, ahp in Cambodia, krasue in Thailand, kasu in Laos, and so on."

I've never heard of such a thing, but I'm instantly obsessed. And I'm reminded once again why Maddie and I love to travel so much. There's really nothing like seeing other parts of the world, exploring new cities, trying new foods, learning about other cultures. That's why we jumped at the chance to fly to Malaysia on a single night's notice. Well, that and the price.

Apparently I do manage to fall asleep, because the next thing I know, I'm waking up to the sound of the pilot informing us that we're making our initial descent into Penang. Maddie wakes up, too, but seems far more refreshed than I feel. Soon we're on the ground, and stepping out into the hair dryer heat of the Malaysian sun. Neither of us has ever felt anything like it, and soon we're both soaked in sweat.

We take a taxi into the George Town section of Penang, where our accommodations are. It's a "guest house", whatever that means. Maddie managed to find the place last night somehow, and booked the last available room, which was only possible because of someone else's last-minute cancellation.

When we arrive, the front door is locked. We ring the bell, but have to wait several minutes in the blazing sun before someone answers. Finally the lock turns and the door creaks open, and we enter the lobby—a small room with tile floors, a bench, a desk, and a few plants. The owner greets us, already knowing our names from the reservation. He doesn't introduce himself, though.

Maddie and I both sigh at the cooler air inside.

"Yes, we have air con," the owner says. "It's nice outside today, though. Warm, but not too hot." We both chuckle, and I secretly wonder if we're going to survive the week.

We go to our room, which is tiny, but perfectly fine, and strip off our wet clothes, then collapse onto the cool sheets of the four-poster bed. Without realizing that it's happening, I instantly crash out again, and enter a dream in which I see a beautiful penanggalan zigzagging across a sheet of ice, almost like a skater, but leaving a slick trail of blood in her path as her intestines drag sloppily behind her. She smiles and stares deep into my eyes as she weaves her way toward me. Then, just as she's about to lunge in my direction, her sharp teeth bared, I'm jolted awake, and surprised to find that it's now late afternoon.

"Come on, babe," Maddie says. "We didn't fly all the way here to just take naps."

I apologize and clear my eyes. In a matter of minutes, we're both up and dressed in fresh clothes and heading back out. The sun is still oppressive, but I almost feel as if I'm getting used to it already. Unless that's just wishful thinking. It probably is.

We choose a direction without looking at a map, and decide to go exploring.

The sidewalks, if you can call them that, are an

adventure in and of themselves. They vary in height, width, and surface type. Close attention must be paid to where each step is set down, unless you want to turn an ankle or fall into an uncovered sewer trench. Some of the walkways are covered by the awnings or roofs of shops. Others have steps or slopes. Some are in ruins; others are tiled and neatly kept. There are gaps and holes, only about half of which are covered by metal grates. Quite often there is very little space to move, and two people cannot stroll casually side-by-side. We've only been walking for a few minutes and more than once we've run into clusters of motorbikes parked in the walkways, blocking foot traffic and forcing us into the streets.

The sun sets, and we're hoping for some relief from the heat, but I imagine it will be another hour or two before we can tell a difference. We continue walking across the city, simply seeing whatever there is to see, and taking pictures without trying to look too much like a couple of clueless tourists.

The air smells fantastic—a mix of incense and street food.

Each storefront we pass appears to be a small business of some sort, and most of them are already closed for the day. We do see a man operating a small printing press inside one of them, and there is an active pizza shop with a painting on the wall of a cat wearing a Darth Vader helmet and holding a slice in one paw. We see signs for civet coffee everywhere and we discuss whether or not we want to drink something that's already run through an animal's digestive system. I'm willing; Maddie isn't.

We discover numerous examples of Penang's street art scene. One artist in particular has created a number of murals that also incorporate real-world objects. A pair of children painted on one wall "ride" the real bicycle installed in front of the building. A painted child "standing" on a real chair reaches up toward a hole in the wall, where an actual orange sits. And another painting shows a child ordering food from a street vendor, while his companion "sits" on a nearby three-dimensional bench. And so on. I spot one mural from down the street that looks like it must be a depiction of a penanggalan, and I get excited, but by the time we reach it, I realize it's just a painting of some oversized fruit.

We pass a Hindu temple and gasp at the astonishing beauty of the brightly-colored sculptures piled high, towering over the street. It's a stunning sight, stacks of human and animal figures painted bright pink and blue and gold and green, all lit up with a heavenly glow against the now-dark sky.

We continue walking, and stumble upon an open-air food court. There are dozens of vendors and what must be at least a hundred tables, all surrounding a stage in the center. There's a roof, but it's held up by pillars instead of walls. A woman sings from the stage, filling the air with a language I don't understand, though I can certainly appreciate its beauty.

We decide we better eat. There's a red and yellow sign over one vendor's space advertising their Obama Vegetarian Spring Rolls, but we opt for something more traditional: the nasi lemak, a coconut rice dish. A woman comes around to take drink orders, then brings us a couple beers, and we sit and enjoy the scene for a while.

Eventually, though, the singing stops and the vendors begin closing up. We realize more time has passed than we thought, so we pack up and set out on foot once again.

Maddie asks which direction I want to head in, and I tell her in a goofy-ghoulish tone that it doesn't matter to me, as long as we keep our eyes peeled for a penanggalan.

She doesn't know what I'm talking about, and I realize I never told her about the book I found on the plane. This reminds me that I left the book behind. I had meant to hold onto it. Damn.

Then she reaches into her bag and produces a small leather-bound tome.

"Is this what you're talking about?" she asks, informing me that she grabbed it from my lap on the plane, when I was asleep and it looked like it might fall to the floor.

I'm overjoyed, and I take it from her, flipping to the center of the book to find the page that features my beloved penanggalan, now the unwitting mascot of our trip. But I can't find it. Somehow it's missing from the book, even though no pages seem to have been removed. It's simply not there anymore, among the other creatures and spirits. I'm confused, but I stuff the book into my back pocket anyway, and describe the strange and beautiful monster as best I can while we walk the streets without any particular destination in mind.

Maddie isn't quite as taken with the penanggalan as I am, but she's not exactly the folklore fanatic I am either. I can't help but feel that if I could show her the illustration in the book, she would understand. Maybe I just overlooked it. I'll flip through the pages again once we're back at the guest house, or we'll find the penanggalan online.

Lost in conversation, we suddenly realize we don't know exactly what part of town we're in. It certainly doesn't feature much nightlife. Soon we get our bearings and we double back in the general direction of where we're staying.

I stumble over some loose chunks of the sidewalk just as Maddie narrowly avoids falling into a trench. The same thing happens again a minute later, so we decide to detour a block over. When we turn the corner, the street opens up a bit wider. We don't encounter any people, but up ahead we see a pair of dogs resting on the sidewalk. We actually think they're statues at first, decoratively guarding a shopfront, but they stir at our approach, and we realize we need to cross the street so as not to rouse them.

That doesn't matter, though. The dogs are instantly aware of us, and not at all happy about our presence. Even though we've given them plenty of space, they clearly think we've intruded on their territory. They growl deeply at first, then begin barking. Maddie and I pick up our pace, speed-walking, just trying to move down the block as quickly as we can so we can find our way back in for the night. It makes no difference. The dogs bark even louder, and suddenly bolt in our direction.

I see now that they're completely untethered. There are no leashes or chains, no barrier of any kind to keep them from us. We need to move.

"Run!" I say, hesitating to make sure Maddie can go ahead of me. Instead, she gives me a push on the shoulder.

"Just go!" she yells. "Don't wait for me!"

So I move, dashing as quickly as I can toward the end of the block. In the moment, I figure that if nothing else, maybe I can at least lure the dogs away from Maddie, and she can find a path to safety for herself. Once I get a certain distance away from the dogs' post, they'll surely leave me be.

But for now, they're angry. And loud. And right on my heels, barking and snarling at our trespass.

I turn back to see how close they are, swearing I can feel the heat of their breath, and also needing to see if Maddie's been able to turn off somewhere. The dogs are right there, but I'm almost to the corner, so I hit the brakes and slide, the soles of my shoes scratching across the dirty pavement as I curl around the bend. I keep my balance, just barely, and make the turn. And just then, there's a loud squeal that rises up above the barking of the dogs.

The stench of vinegar pierces my nostrils, which doesn't make sense at first, until I fully round the corner. That's when I see her. Not Maddie, but her. Her beautiful face, her long black hair. Her dangling blood-slicked viscera.

The penanggalan.

An otherworldly light seems to illuminate her with an almost unnatural glow. She smiles at me, and I feel a warmth inside, much hotter than the heat of the Malaysian sun.

Her gaze locks onto mine, and I feel my eyes widen. The odor of vinegar hits me again, as she lunges for me, smiling, her mouth opening wide, and I see the foul cluster of internal organs—lungs, heart, stomach, intestines—hanging beneath her neck, a heap of soft, twisted entrails. So lovely. I get lost in her eyes and the black void between the rows of her pointed teeth, and she's everything to me in that moment.

I feel the bite. The smell of vinegar is overpowering. The intersection lights up, and the dogs have disappeared, and everything feels like a blooming flower. I feel a breeze, and the temperature plummets, and suddenly everything turns to red.

•••••••••••

"I don't know," Maddie says. "It all happened so quickly. We were walking, and all of a sudden these dogs came after us. We tried to get away, but they were so fast. I told him not to wait for me, and he ran ahead, and when he turned the corner, this car just came from out of nowhere and..."

A woman, the driver, sits on a bench in the next room, sobbing, her tear-drenched eyes covered by her long black hair. She holds a hand firmly to her chest, just beneath her neck, in an effort to calm herself.

Down the hall, a doctor emerges and addresses a police officer.

"I've never seen anything like it before," he says. "The impact split him open like an overripe piece of fruit. The entire rib cage burst outward, and all his internal organs spilled, en masse, onto the pavement." The doctor pauses, then hands the officer a small black book. "This was in his back pocket," he says. "Maybe his wife will want it."

The officer flips the book open about halfway, to a page folded in toward the center.

"Terrible," he says, shaking his head. "But at least it was a quick death. Although I always wonder how much of what happened actually registered in the victim's mind."

He and the doctor part ways, and the officer unfolds the page in the center of the book. He is taken with the depiction of the beautiful woman there, her piercing eyes, her lovely long black hair.

He snaps the book shut and stuffs it into his back pocket, then decides to go outside for some air. As he steps through the doorway, he takes a deep breath and pauses as a warm breeze hits his face, bringing the smells of the city to his nose—incense, street food, and the slightest hint of vinegar.

CAN'T SEE THE FOREST

Sidney stood there, twisting himself into an unnatural, borderline-painful position, as he tried to examine himself in the toothpaste-speckled mirror. Grasping one shoulder with the opposite hand, he did his best to pull his torso one way while straining to turn his head as far as possible in the other direction.

He leaned against the porcelain sink for leverage, but his body would only twist so far before injury occurred.

He had never noticed anything on his back until a few days earlier. No marks or freckles, no random patches of hair, nothing. Granted, he wasn't in the habit of surveying his own back all that often, but he would catch a glimpse from time to time, usually after a shower, or while grooming.

But that had changed on Monday when he noticed

a small, round spot, positioned just above center, evenly situated between the lower corners of his shoulder blades. It was no larger in diameter than a standard pencil, or perhaps a small green pea, but this was dark brown against his otherwise pasty skin tone.

When the hell did you show up? he'd thought to himself. *And what are you? A freckle? A mole?*

He was running late for work, as he usually was on Monday mornings, having gotten a little too used to two straight days without the screeching of his morning alarm. He'd have to take a closer look at the new growth later.

Each morning since then, he'd taken a few extra moments to examine the spot on his back as best he could, since he tended to forget about it over the course of each day, as he got wrapped up in things at work.

His job had been consuming the majority of both his time and mental real estate these days, with his bosses making increasingly unrealistic demands of the staff, and more and more of his colleagues calling out sick and, in some cases, never returning. Not to mention the growing hordes of protestors that had been showing up outside the building lately.

It wasn't easy to get a good look at the thing on his back, given its placement, but he felt he could see it a little better with each passing day. Perhaps he should stretch more often. Julie, his ex, had extolled the virtues of her yoga routine the entire eight months they'd been together, although Sid had never expressed much interest. *Maybe she was onto something,* he thought.

Was the mole bigger today? It was Friday now. Maybe the stress of the week was just getting to him, but Sidney could swear the thing looked a little larger. Not much. Just slightly. There was no way to tell for sure. It wasn't as if he'd taken a ruler to the spot upon first noticing it. The mark did seem slightly raised, however. Maybe he just hadn't observed that aspect of the mole before.

He was also convinced now that it was indeed a mole, and not a freckle. *Freckles aren't raised at all,* he told himself. *That was true, wasn't it?*

••••••••••••

At work, Sidney shifted around in his chair uncomfortably all day. Several times the plasticky faux-leather crunched in ways that brought him unwanted attention, his coworkers shooting disapproving glances in his direction, or at least furrowing their brows while doing their best not to look his way.

At various points, he felt discomfort in the middle of his back. He sensed pressure when he leaned back, and the slightest bit of relief when he adjusted his posture to sit up straighter. *Was this something he needed to see a doctor about?* He imagined he would probably be referred to a dermatologist, which meant not just one but two separate appointments, something he really didn't have time for.

Too many of his colleagues simply weren't showing up anymore, and the company wasn't hiring new people fast enough. Managers stood in their offices and conference rooms, huddled and whispering like the heads of some shadowy criminal organization. It was just a furniture company, though. Granted, it was one of the largest in the world, and it was far from being a morally-centered company, but still. Whatever was going on, Sidney hoped it was temporary, and he hoped they would hire some new people soon. His daily duties had been increasing for a while now.

If he did have to take a day or two off to see doctors, though, then so be it. At least that would be one or two days he didn't have to swim through the sea of protestors outside. He understood they were passionate about what they believed in, but what could he do about it? He just worked in the shipping department. It wasn't like he was out there with a chainsaw, cutting down the forests himself. He wasn't in the factories using the chemicals they used. He simply arranged for the company's products to get around the country so customers could purchase them. At least, that's what he was trying to do. Each day lately, his workload seemed a little more frustrating and difficult than it had been the day before.

He huffed, doing his best to put these thoughts out of his mind and instead focus on his immediate work. He was only a few hours away from another weekend, if he could manage to finish his tasks as quickly as he hoped.

•••••••••••••

He had a date scheduled for Saturday—with Monica, whom he'd met online. Friday night, however, he had to himself. At one point in Sidney's life, Friday nights had been for hanging with the boys, playing video games while drinking far too much, and things of that sort. But most of his friends were married now, with fatherly responsibilities, and so drunken, wasted Friday nights with them were a thing of the past.

These days, he liked to order pizza and watch a movie, sometimes two, on his own—usually something involving high stakes action and a plethora of sizeable explosions.

When the pizza arrived, he set it down on the coffee table between the couch and TV, opened the cardboard box and inhaled the delightful aromas of tomato sauce, cheese, onions, and peppers before grabbing the remote and choosing something to watch.

It didn't take him long to find the latest in a long line of car chase movies available for rental, so he selected the button to start the evening's entertainment, then tugged a piece of pizza away from the rest of the pie and sat back, holding the sagging slice aloft before sliding the pointed end between his teeth.

He nearly choked as he leaned against the couch cushions and felt a stabbing sensation in the middle of his back. He winced, making a sound through his mouthful of food, then bounced forward as he tried to reach the center of his back with his fingertips. He knew exactly what it was, though. It wasn't anything to do with the couch. It was the mole.

He swallowed and dropped the remainder of his slice back into the wedge-shaped void in the box, then made his way to the bathroom, leaving the movie playing in the background.

The light over the mirror flickered when he flipped the switch. *Great, something else to worry about,* Sidney thought. He'd just had to replace his kitchen garbage disposal a couple weeks ago, and now this. After a few seconds, though, the light glowed solidly. Maybe it was just the bulb.

He reached over his head and pulled his shirt up and

off from the back of its collar. On the way up, he felt a twinge of pain, as if the shirt had gotten snagged. *Had the mole grown even more already?* he wondered, his thoughts suddenly racing to all sorts of unpleasant possibilities. He didn't have time for this shit.

He dropped the shirt to the floor and spun around, twisting his body just as he had every other day this week, to get a better view.

And sure enough, the mole was larger. Not so much in terms of its diameter—that aspect remained about the size of a pea—but the thing seemed taller now, rising what appeared to be a quarter-inch or so off the otherwise flat surface of his back.

Worse than that, however, was the fact that beside the mole sat two more dark spots, one a lighter brown, the other medium gray in color.

He cursed at his own reflection. He'd definitely have to see a doctor now. Inconvenient as that was, there was clearly something going on with his body that needed to be addressed.

He let go of his shoulder and tried instead to reach up to the center of his back from below, snaking an arm up beneath its own armpit and stretching to reach the problem area. He couldn't quite find it, though. The mole, and now these two new spots, seemed to be in the one area of his back he wasn't able to touch with his fingers.

He gave up his attempt, frustrated, and resolved to call his doctor the next morning, although he couldn't remember if they had weekend hours. He didn't think so.

His stomach gurgled, reminding him of the pizza cooling in the other room, and the movie he had forgotten to pause. He put his shirt back on carefully and returned to the living room, where he stopped the movie, took another bite of his food, then went to the kitchen, where he poured himself a glass of soda before adding a hearty amount of bourbon to it.

He sat back down on the couch, making sure to lean forward, and started the movie over, so that he could pay full attention to the opening chase scene. Despite his uncomfortable position, he managed to forget about the mole and its new companions for a little while.

When the movie concluded, his stomach gurgled even louder than it had two hours earlier, and he realized he had eaten three-quarters of the large pizza. He cradled the underside of his protruding belly with one arm and decided to clean up and go to bed.

•••••••••••••

Had he really poured that much bourbon into his drink? Upon waking the next morning, Sidney found himself face down against a fitted sheet that desperately needed to be washed, and experiencing a terrible, throbbing headache, with pain radiating down his neck. The birds chirping outside weren't helping matters.

His head had rolled off the pillow at some point in the night, which he figured might be to blame for some of the soreness. He hoped that getting up and moving around would help.

From his prone position, Sidney dragged his left arm along the mattress until he reached the base of his skull with his palm. He squeezed the muscles there, then slid his hand further down his neck. He remembered something Julie had told him once about pressure points and wondered if he was doing it right.

A few inches down, where his neck met his shoulders, he felt a series of tiny bumps. His eyes shot open but focused on nothing in particular as he tried to visualize what he was touching. He ran his fingers over the uneven texture. There had to be at least a dozen small mounds just on the lower part of his neck, each of them rising noticeably from the surface of his skin. They continued even more densely farther down.

He pressed into one of them, gently. It was firm, but squished under the pressure, feeling almost like a rubber eraser.

Sidney felt nauseous. He struggled to press himself up from the mattress, but managed despite the stiffness in his neck, and now, he realized, in his back as well. When he reached the bathroom, he flipped the light switch and waited a moment while the bulb flickered to life overhead.

He didn't need to remove his shirt to see how much worse things had gotten overnight.

His neck and back were covered with numerous bulges. Between his shoulder blades, where the first mole had appeared, there were now several spires rising at least two inches off his back, poking their now-tapered ends through the fabric of his t-shirt. And there were smaller bumps in places they hadn't been just a few hours earlier, when he had crawled into bed.

He peeled his shirt off carefully, feeling sharp twinges of pain as the tips of the moles—or whatever they were—snagged the cotton fabric.

Examining himself in the dingy mirror, he could

see what had to be a hundred new growths spreading in all directions across his back. They varied slightly in size, though most had the same diameter as the first, and they appeared in a range of earthy colors, from browns and grays to maroon and rusty orange, as well as a few that were more of a dark mustard yellow.

The initial grouping between his shoulder blades were the tallest of all, and, like some of the others, were pointed. They seemed stiffer now too, or at least looked that way, though he still couldn't quite reach them with his fingertips to be sure. And there was something else—the tallest moles seemed to have tiny spikes growing out from their sides.

They looked like…little trees.

What the fuck?! Sidney felt a wave of coolness pass over his forehead. A sheen of sweat began to form all over his body. He didn't know what this was, but it couldn't possibly be benign.

He ran back to the bedroom to retrieve his phone. The screen instantly lit up with a text from one of his managers, asking if he would be able to come into work. *I know it's Saturday*, it read, *but 2/3 of the staff called out. We need bodies in here. Use the back entrance. Thx.*

Sidney replied with a quick *I'm sick*, to which there was no response. Then he opened his Contacts and pulled up his doctor's number.

The line trilled four times before an answering service picked up, at which point he was informed that the doctor was on vacation for another nine days.

Without going into too much embarrassing detail, Sidney explained that he had some sort of growth on his back that he needed someone to look at. He felt it was an emergency situation, but the person on the line didn't seem terribly understanding or sympathetic. He asked if he could get a referral to a dermatologist over the phone, but was told he would have to wait for someone to get back to him. They hoped it would be today, but couldn't make any promises, since the doctor was traveling and difficult to reach.

He ended the call and angrily threw the phone straight down onto the bed, where it bounced straight up, as if on a trampoline, before flopping over.

What was he going to do?

He turned on the TV, just for the noise, but a news anchor was reporting on the people protesting his company's refusal to acknowledge its role in a slew of environmental concerns, so he shut it off immediately. He didn't need the stress of his job in the background while he dealt with the stress of whatever what happening to his body.

He went to the kitchen next and poured himself a splash of bourbon, hoping a little hair-of-the-dog might ease his headache somewhat, or at least calm his nerves. *It was worth a shot*, he thought, *so to speak*.

The back of his throat tingled as the bourbon went down, a welcome sensation. He immediately felt warm inside.

Returning to the bedroom to retrieve his phone, he texted Monica to let her know he was sick and would have to cancel their date. *Maybe next weekend*, he offered, hoping his life would be back to normal by then. It seemed like wishful thinking, but he had to hope.

•••••••••••••

By early evening, Sidney could no longer stand up straight. The weight of the many growths on his back had become almost too much to support. He moved about the house slowly, hunched over, bracing himself on railings and the corners of furniture. He was unable to sit anywhere or even wear a shirt without pain.

He took another look in the mirror. There were even more of them now. They had spread down and across the small of his back, and he could feel several little lumps beginning to form along the tops of his buttocks. They had started to curl their way around his sides, in rows tracing the paths of his ribs. And they had begun crawling over his shoulders and further around the sides of his neck, sprouting from his trapezius muscles, the tops of his shoulders, even the backs of his arms.

And, as before, the earliest ones had grown taller. The first cluster of moles were now four or five inches tall, with the next batch radiating outward standing at least half that height. They also had little spikes now, like branches, growing out in all directions.

Sidney's stomach gurgled as if in response to his appearance, and he lurched, nearly vomiting. He looked monstrous.

He exited the bathroom, no longer able to bear the sight of his own reflection.

He hadn't gotten any response from the doctor about a referral, so he tried calling again, but this time, there was neither any answer nor the option to leave a message. Even more frustrated, he threw the phone again, this time against the wall. He heard the device crunch upon impact with the drywall and then the floor, but was too angry and exhausted to investigate how bad the damage was.

Instead, he convinced himself to eat something. Even though he wasn't hungry, he knew he needed the fuel, if only for the energy to transport the extra weight that had formed so mysteriously on his body in just a matter of days, and which had multiplied so greatly in just hours.

He passed over the last couple slices of pizza and instead forced down some leftovers from earlier in the week, but they turned his stomach immediately, and he began feeling even more ill than he already did. He threw up into the kitchen sink within moments, and instantly felt the hollowness in his belly.

Water. He knew he needed water, and that he could most likely keep it down. He poured himself a glass from the pitcher in the fridge and chugged it, then repeated the effort. He refilled the pitcher, but found himself too impatient to wait for it to filter, so he filled his glass from the faucet and drank that too. It helped.

Was he dying? he wondered. *Was this some strange new disease that hadn't made headlines yet? Was it something even worse?* He had to see a doctor, had to figure out what was happening.

He resolved to go to the hospital. He considered driving himself, then realized how unlikely it was that he would be able to operate a car in his condition.

He returned to the bedroom to find his phone so he could call 911, but when he picked it up from the wooden floor, the newly-spiderwebbed screen would no longer light up.

He felt woozy. *Was he about to faint?* He told himself no, refusing to pass out. He could muscle through this one way or another. He'd see a doctor, though not his own—

if not tonight than certainly tomorrow, or Monday at the absolute latest, even though his absence at the office would surely cause an even further backlog of work. But it's not as if he was the only one calling out. *And he simply had to see someone about this, didn't he?* They'd figure out what was happening. Some dermatologist would assess the situation, freeze and remove the moles, and before long, Sidney would be able to go on with his life as if nothing had ever happened. Even if he was out all day Monday he'd be able to catch up at work with a couple late nights over the course of the week. *So what if some couches or dining tables showed up at their respective locations a day or two late?* And with any luck, maybe he would be able to make that date with Monica next weekend after all.

He turned on the ceiling fan over the bed to cool the room.

He stretched up and backward as far as he could, attempting to stand straighter, but it was useless. He could hear his back and sides creak, and waves of pain shot through his entire body, starting from the spot between his shoulder blades where the first mole had appeared less than a week ago.

Finally he collapsed on the bed, once again face down on the dirty sheets, because it was the only way he could possibly lay. Within moments, he passed out.

•••••••••••

Sidney didn't wake until many hours later. It was very late at night—he knew that much—but he wasn't able to turn his head to see the clock on the dresser across the room.

He felt terrible—even stiffer than before, feverish,

achy, swollen. His mouth was dry. He needed water, but wasn't sure he could make it to the kitchen. He wasn't even sure he could stand up.

He felt the breeze from the ceiling fan. At least there was that, he thought. The cool air felt nice, a small gift he relished.

He heard something then. A strange whooshing, rustling sound. It was somewhat rhythmic. It wasn't just the spinning of the fan blades, nor was it the fan's motor, which had always been relatively silent. No, this was something else.

The way his head was turned to the side, somewhat propped up by the pillow from behind, he was able to see his left shoulder and a portion of his back, just beyond it. Even in the low light he could see the outlines of the growths that covered him now—the moles, or whatever they were. They were even taller than they had been the last time he looked. And it seemed they had all sprouted tiny arms from their various, multicolored trunks. Each one of the tiny trees had grown branches. Not only that, but the branches now had leaves.

That's what the noise was. The rustling of tiny leaves in the wind from the fan.

It was an oddly soothing sound, like a cushion of static, or the velvety sound of ocean waves crashing. He remembered the week he and Julie had spent at her father's house on the Cape, how relaxing it had been. He wondered if he'd ever get to do something like that again.

The sound seemed almost as if it was getting louder in the room. Or perhaps he was just focusing on it. Either way, he felt himself start to drift back to sleep. It was just as well, he thought, since he didn't feel capable of movement, and didn't know what he would do even if he could get out of bed.

As he began to fall back into unconsciousness, a calmness washed over him just like the cool breeze blowing through the little trees.

It was only interrupted by the vaguest sensation— something he felt, just barely, from the small of his back. He twitched. At first, he thought he had begun drifting again into sleep, only to be jolted by the feeling of falling. But he quickly realized this was something else.

Footsteps. Tiny, almost imperceptible footsteps in the miniature forest, creeping from the far edge of the growths on his back. He felt them move, cautiously, left-right-left-right, in a line from the lower part of his back, up his spine, to the space between his shoulder blades. They stopped there. And waited.

He felt more of them too. A series of footsteps from his right shoulder, another from between the ribs on his left side, another stepping out from the little hairs on the back of his neck. And another, and another, and another. They all took paths to the center of his back, just as the first one had, all moving to congregate at the exact place where that very first mole had appeared. That very first little tree.

He felt ten, maybe twelve different sets of footsteps lead to that spot, and all stop.

And then, in the still of the night, in the darkness, as he lay face down on the bed, just beneath the sounds of the wind and the rustling leaves, he heard whispers.

Sidney could only hear a portion of the conversation, enough to know it was about him. But it was bigger than that. Everything was going according to plan, one of the tiny creatures was saying. The testing phase had gone well. Now it was time to expand their operation.

THE NOISE MACHINE

Dave and I weren't friends per se, but we talked from time to time. His yard butts up against mine, and we would see each other outside on occasion. Sometimes he would ask for a hand moving something heavy, or I'd borrow some tools from him. It was a very neighborly relationship—the kind where neither of us would invade each other's personal life or space too deeply, but we'd also keep an eye out for one another.

I knew he was a widower, like me, but we never discussed it. I never saw any evidence of children.

He was a tinkerer too. He had even built an addition onto the back of his house, to serve as a workshop.

One day, Dave told me he was having trouble sleeping at night. With a smile, I suggested counting sheep, before more seriously furthering the idea into talk of meditation, but he seemed skeptical. I then suggested a noise machine—one of those things with prerecorded loops of static, or ocean waves, or the sounds of the tropical rainforest. I'd had one for my kids when they were little, and it was a godsend.

Living on the outskirts of the city, there's always some level of noise outside, like the hum of passing traffic or neighbors calling to one another from opposite ends of the block. Many people find it comforting, while others just think of it as a distraction after a certain hour of the night. For some, the sound of white noise can help calm the mind.

Anyway, Dave was open to the idea of a noise machine, and he decided to give one a try—the exact model I suggested, actually. It didn't work for him, though. Later, he told me he ended up test-driving a few different brands, but still wasn't getting much rest. I could see it in his eyes, not to mention the bags beneath them.

He believed in the idea of it, however, and was much more open to it than taking some sort of pill. So he decided to go about building one of his own.

Like I said, Dave was a tinkering sort of fellow. Always had been, from what he told me on a few occasions. As a boy, he used to mess with radios, walkie talkies, and so on, rigging the electronics in different ways, always trying to build something new. I guess that's why he was so critical of the store-bought noise machines. He must've felt like he could build a better one himself.

I didn't see Dave for a while after that, although I certainly heard him. From my backyard, I could hear metal clanging, and the sounds of drills and hammers. I wondered if he was working on his noise machine or some other project in that workshop of his.

A couple weeks later, I finally saw Dave in the flesh again, and asked how he was doing. He was enthusiastically upbeat, and looked far better rested. I was happy for him.

He thanked me for suggesting the noise machine. While the commercially-available options didn't work out for him, the idea led him down a path of invention, and the one he had built himself was, as he put it, a miracle.

He asked if I'd like to come over and check it out.

I had never been inside Dave's house prior to that day. Again, we were neighbors, but not really friends. He brought me in through the back, where I got to see his workshop. It was impressive, but messy, with cardboard boxes and plastic bins of junk stacked everywhere and tools scattered across every surface. All sorts of objects hung on the pegboard walls. It looked more like an indoor junkyard, but I had the impression Dave knew where anything he might need would be located. I was terrified I would knock something over as I made my way through, or step on some crucial element of a project he was working on.

He asked if I wanted something to drink, but I declined, then we made our way upstairs. The house was quiet, except for the sounds of the street outside.

Dave lived alone. As I mentioned, I had heard he was married once, and that his wife had passed, but I never felt like asking about too many personal details. I spotted a photo on the wall along the stairs, which I assumed was her. She had long dark hair; from the style of it, I assumed the photo was at least twenty years old.

He led me into his bedroom, and positioned himself on one side of the space, opposite the noise machine. He gestured toward it with one hand before I even entered the room, beaming with pride. I focused on his massive grin as I stepped through the doorway, then turned to behold his creation.

I had expected something small, like a box that would fit on a nightstand, or perhaps on the floor beside the bed. But this thing he had built, this elaborate machine, was an absolute monstrosity! It took up the entire wall, from corner to corner and floor to ceiling. It looked like some ancient computer built at a university, with what looked like hundreds of buttons and dials, even a few small video screens. I was surprised and impressed, and maybe a little frightened.

Dave could tell the sheer enormity of it had thrown me. He quickly explained that he didn't like the poor sound quality in the commercial versions he had tried, and didn't like the fact that they just used loops of the same stretch of sound, ranging anywhere from ten to thirty seconds long. His machine was much more advanced. It created new electronic sounds in real time, with tiny variations, and it kept creating new noise, as opposed to playing prerecorded sound. This, for him at least, was far better.

He told me to have a seat, then he stepped over to the machine. There was a soft hum in the air the moment he flipped the first switch, and it grew from there. Within a few minutes, after a number of dial adjustments, the room was filled with warm, comforting static. To say that it was impressive wouldn't do the moment—or Dave's work— justice.

Dave described, in a very loud voice (though it was still difficult to catch every word), some of the tweaks that could be made with the machine, to alter the type of sound desired for any given night. He explained that turning certain dials one way would help to cover up the sounds of voices from outside, while other settings could dampen car noise, or music, or the sounds of nocturnal animals milling about in the dark. He even had a special setting that would cancel out the sounds of fireworks.

Not being very technologically-minded, I didn't fully understand everything he was telling me, but I was still struck by it all. We spent a few minutes with the noise—I even began to feel a bit drowsy—and then he lowered the volume, before turning the machine off entirely. He said he had some work to do, and I told him I had plans that night anyway, so he walked me back downstairs and I exited. I was careful not to step on anything as I walked back through his shambles of a workshop on the way out.

Another week passed before I saw Dave again. I was doing some yard work, and he was returning home from the store. He had a dozen or so bags, which all seemed to be filled with snacks—pretzels, potato chips, and the like—and I asked if he was throwing a party. I immediately regretted asking. If he was, I obviously hadn't been invited.

But he said there was no party, and that the contents of his shopping bags were for his noise machine. I must have displayed an obvious look of puzzlement, because he chuckled, then waved me over.

He told me he had made some more adjustments to his machine, and he'd like to show me. So for the second time, Dave led me inside and upstairs. When I stepped into his bedroom, my eyes nearly fell out of my head.

The machine had tripled in size. It took up most of the room now, leaving only enough space for his bed in one corner. He had moved his other furniture—a dresser, a mirror, a small bookcase, a nightstand, and a chair—out into the hallway.

I stood, mouth agape, admiring the massive construction, and he chuckled again. Then he started pointing out some of the new features. He explained that after a while, he had reached the conclusion that the electronically-produced sounds the machine was making weren't quite good enough. He still used them, of course, but he had decided to incorporate other elements too.

There was now a section of the machine that held water inside a small glass tank, creating its own miniature rainfall. Another contraption had a pair of robotic hands that crunched up sheets of aluminum foil and then flattened them back out before balling them up again. There was a part of the machine that incorporated an old television, which displayed a salt and pepper static screen like I hadn't seen in years. There was a tumbler that kept a pile of gravel in perpetual motion. Another section acted as a sort of press, slowly crunching piles of chips and pretzels, which were fed through a wide tube off to the side.

This was the moment I began wondering if Dave was perhaps a bit mad. Sure, this thing he had created was impressive, but was it all necessary? It was certainly eccentric, if nothing else.

Dave was beaming about his work, and I made sure to compliment him numerous times, but I felt a sudden urge to leave. I made up some excuse—I can't remember what now—and went back home.

I didn't see him again for a while. On days I spent time outside, I could hear more of Dave's workshop sounds: sheets of metal being forced into certain shapes, holes being drilled, nails being hammered.

Soon I began hearing the noise machine itself. I supposed he was just running tests, perhaps making some more tweaks and adjustments. *Who knows,* I thought, *maybe he's adding even more components to it!* There was only so much space in that room, though—at a certain point, he'd have to make some decisions about what to include and what not to.

Eventually, I could hear the noise machine with regularity. Before long, the sound of several forms of interwoven static was constant, even from within my own house with the doors and windows closed. It was distant enough that it didn't bother me too much, but it was still very much present. I think it must have even helped me sleep a little better at night, drowning out some of the other noises from the neighborhood.

Another week passed. The noise coming from Dave's house had remained constant, and was becoming more prominent each day. I hadn't seen him in some time, but considered knocking just to make sure he was okay, and that he hadn't lost himself in a maze of new components for his creation.

I overheard a few other neighbors on the sidewalk talking about the noise. One was on her phone, quite upset, seemingly speaking to the police about the matter, while others stood on the street, pointing toward Dave's house, raising their arms and voices, complaining to each other.

I began to notice some more localized sounds from inside my own house too—small tinkling and buzzing sounds—and I realized that my walls and floors were vibrating. Plates and dishes had begun skittering across my kitchen countertop, and on occasion, various trinkets would fall from their shelves.

The noise from Dave's house continued to grow louder with each passing day. If the complaint made by our one neighbor had actually resulted in a visit from the police, they certainly hadn't convinced Dave to change his ways.

One night, the lights went out in the neighborhood. I immediately wondered if Dave's machine had been drawing too much power and somehow shut down our part of the grid. The entire area went black and quiet. Except for the noise, that is. Somehow, the sounds of fuzzy, crinkling static persisted. I wondered if Dave had set up his own generator.

I grabbed a flashlight and made my way over to Dave's house. I knocked at the back, and the workshop door fell open. The sounds from inside intensified. I could hear amplified static, along with the smashing of pretzels, the dribbling of water, piles of rocks knocking and grinding against each other.

I stepped in and found his workshop to be even more of a mess than before.

As I moved deeper into the house, panning my flashlight back and forth, I found the rooms of the first floor to be filled with haphazardly-stacked furniture, some of which I recalled seeing in the hallway upstairs the last time I visited.

I called out for Dave, but there was surely no way he would be able to hear me through the noise. I could barely hear my own voice through the humming, buzzing, crunching cacophony.

I started up the stairs, flashlight in one hand. As I cupped my other hand over one of my ears, I noticed that the photo I assumed was Dave's wife had fallen off its nail.

The hallway was trashed, and the sound was more intense the closer I got to Dave's bedroom. I called his name several more times, but it was pointless.

Finally, I reached the bedroom and gasped. The door had been pulled from its hinges and now lay flat on the hall floor like a welcome mat. The machine inside had grown even larger since I'd last seen it. It spilled into the center of the room now. There were even components dangling from the ceiling. Everything was abuzz. I could feel the sound waves in the air around me, tickling my body hair and rattling my eardrums. I could feel it on my skin. I could feel it in my chest.

The bed was gone. Now, in the center of the room, beneath various scraps of metal, and tangled in a series of wires and cables, lay Dave. He was face down, his body pointing toward the doorway, and he was severely bruised and cut, but still alive. He lurched upward, raising his head, and I could immediately see the damage to his face. Where his eyes should have been, there were now only dark voids. Blood had spilled from both of his ruined ears, down the sides of his head and neck, and onto his shoulders.

Sensing my presence, he reached out as best he could through the tangled mass of cords with one arm. I shined the light on his face and saw him mouth the word "help", although I couldn't actually hear it through the noise. Then the wires surrounding him tightened, reeling his arm back in toward his body and pulling him flat against the floor.

To my right, I sensed movement, so I swung the light in that direction. To my horror, the machine itself was moving. The side panels heaved as if the thing was breathing. The robotic arms I had previously seen balling up sheets of foil were longer and bulkier than they had been before, as if they had grown metallic, wiry muscles. They reached out and swiped at me, but I was luckily out of their range. Hundreds, maybe thousands of dials and levers moved on their own. The metal frame of the machine even seemed to be expanding—actually growing—and it suddenly smashed its way through the wall to the left of the doorway.

I screamed but couldn't hear it.

Somehow, I managed to leap over the writhing, twisting, expanding components of the machine and dashed out of the room. I ran down the hall just before it crashed through the rest of the bedroom's walls. Vibrating with fear and confusion, I glanced back when I reached the top of the stairs and saw the machine quickly take over the entire second floor of the house, its metal plates unfolding and expanding, wires spreading like time-lapse nature footage, metallic arms launching through any obstructions, lights flickering and speakers blaring as they hurtled toward me.

The sound was more intense than ever. I was afraid my eardrums might shatter.

I flew down the stairs, as a series of thick cables punched down through the ceiling of the first floor. They were followed in short order by more metal, which unfolded itself across the drywall before growing its own sets of lights and dials and speakers. I somehow evaded the reach of the wires, and barely escaped the house with my life.

•••••••••••••

Since that night, things have not improved. The noise has never ceased for even a moment, and the machine has not stopped growing. It's taken over several blocks of the neighborhood now, my own house included, and it shows no hint of slowing. It's like a living thing. An evil thing. It seems determined to take over this town, and perhaps stretch its purview even farther.

Many of us have gone deaf in the days since. Some have died. Others sleep constantly and can't seem to be woken. Our pets have run away, somehow able to escape the grasp of the machine's power. Our babies have dehydrated themselves crying. Those of us who still have our hearing can't hear anything *but* the noise, even with earplugs. And I fear it's driving many of us insane.

The machine has begun spitting out clouds of smoke now too, which blot out the sun during the day, as well as the stars at night. None of us have any sense of time anymore.

The electricity returns intermittently, but never for very long, and the soundwaves from the machine seem to have interfered with all things mechanical anyway. I had hoped to type this account into an email and send it everywhere I could think of, but to no avail. Even when we have power, we can no longer operate our computers or phones or appliances. Our generators have failed. Our cars won't run. Each time we move, the machine seems to know, reflexively sprouting even more wires and speakers, growing in whichever direction we attempt to go, boxing us in. We want to escape it but aren't sure we can. Food is growing scarce, and we are struggling to even think clearly most days. Some of us have gone into catatonic states.

And so I've written this all down on scraps of paper with the last pencil I've been able to find, using what may be the final bits of my sanity, and my last moments of clarity. I realize we may never be saved, but I have hope that somehow this account will survive and may one day be discovered. At least then people will know what happened here. Provided there *are* still people, that is.

If you're reading this, then perhaps I was right, and there is still some tiny shred of hope. And if so, then please, carry that hope with you as long as you can.

ACKNOWLEDGEMENTS

Many thanks to Adam Cesare, Aaron Dries, Patrick Lacey, Matt Serafini, Samantha Kolesnik, Aiden Merchant, Julia Lewis, Ben Long, Andrew Robert, and everyone who has ever read and reviewed my work. And, of course, to Gina, my number one fan.

SCOTT COLE is a writer, artist, and graphic designer living in Philadelphia.

Find him on social media, behind you in the mirror, or at **13VISIONS.COM**.

Made in the USA
Middletown, DE
10 July 2022

68991259R00085